Fiona of

Kinsale

Antoinette Berthelotte

It is my honor to dedicate this book to all who supported me, encouraged me and loved me enough to be brutally honest.
Thank you to my husband Doug who learned when to bring me another cup of coffee and when to peek into the office and silently leave me be.
A special thanks to my eagle-eyed sister Peggy, my daughters Robin and Kathleen and to the spirit of my Nana, Margaret Josephine, a real Galway Girl.
I have learned that one is never too old to let their words sing.

DOUBLE FUN PRESS

DOUBLEFUNPRESS@YAHOO.COM

Table of Contents

FORWARD

Fiona Gearaghty's future seemed assured during the summer of 1601. She was still in the bosom of her loving and prosperous family, in a picturesque, protected fishing and trading village on the southern Irish Coast. She had several choices of whom to wed, but no hurry to do so. England now ruled and controlled most of Ireland, except for the lands in the wild north. but there was little change in the lives of the citizens of Kinsale because of it. The failed invasion of England by the Spanish Armada in 1588 was but a distant memory. All of this was to change in the fall as the Spaniard's last Armada, through the capriciousness of winds and weather, put Kinsale in the middle of this historic battle for a free Ireland.

With upheaval and deprivation as a backdrop, Fiona's safe future is cruelly torn from her and she is forced to find a new path while hiding a black secret from those she loved.

LATE AUGUST 1601 – KINSALE, IRELAND

I felt it was cruel to be stuck upstairs choking on the dust created while cleaning. The outside air was clear, and fresh and I could feel it ruffle the light brown curls peeking out of my dust-cap. I wished they were reddish gold like my sister Chloe's. The second story window had a wonderful view of the harbour spread out to the south. The stately ships at anchor and the small fishing boats bobbing about made my feet itch to run down the hill and join them. I could smell the salty air as the breeze through the window began to replace the musty odor of the room. Castle Ni Park Fort on one side of the entrance to the harbour and Ringcurran Castle on the other, both stalwart guardians of Kinsale, were reassuringly visible.

The harbourside, as always, beckoned me with its promised tales of adventure. Perhaps it was the ships coming in with record hauls of fish, wonderful delights from foreign shores, or stories of battles with roving pirates, which made it so appealing. The larger ships waited on the tide to carry them toward the open sea. From there they would find their way to other countries, laden with the much admired Kinsale wine casks and hides. They would leave the safety of the harbour to risk sudden storms on the Atlantic, or the notorious dangers of the English Channel. The smaller craft could be going the same direction to catch large ocean fish or sailing west up the River Bandon for the rich, freshwater angling there.

My thoughts turned pleasantly to the times my father would take me, as a wee lass, with him as he conducted his business on the quay. The rough men on the docks became quite courteous in respect to my father and in deference to my presence. They would touch their forelocks and say something polite. I clearly recall one old man with a grizzled beard who worked for him saying,

"Good day to ye, Master Gearaghty." Would ye mind if I gave yer darlin' girl a sweetie? It's wrapped in paper and as clean as me mother's heart."

Alas, now as a young woman of sixteen, I was no longer taken along to such places and I missed the excitement and spending time with my dear Da.

For now, dreaming of those adventures had to be put aside due to Mother's insistence on the need for a "fearsome cleaning" before winter made us shutter the house once again. All of Kinsale, nestled against the rolling hills, lay at my feet and yet I was burdened with buckets, rags and brooms, my only battles being with a summer's worth of grime and my only haul was to be a prodigious number of cobwebs.

Ten-year-old Chloe and I were currently mucking through our brother's room which was, by far, the dirtiest of the four rooms upstairs. Colum, at thirteen and Robbie, just past fourteen, were not fastidious about their persons, nor their rooms. They managed to track in huge clumps of mud over the summer, which, of course, dried and became a fine layer of dirt which found its way into every crevice and corner. Meg, our housekeeper, and Molly, our kitchen help, kept things under control downstairs, but my parents expected all the children to take responsibility for their own rooms. The boys did the absolute minimum, knowing that when the time came for heavy cleaning, we girls stepped in and the boys made sure they were elsewhere. The clever lads soon learned all they had to do was wait and eventually their room would be cleaned. I had complained to Mam more than once, but she made it clear we girls were the ones who needed to learn how to run a proper household when we wed.

"Hrmmph," I thought, "I suppose Colum and Robbie think the faeries sneak in and clean for them."

I turned to Chloe, who was no happier to be there than I, and told her,

"If we can get this part of the task out of the way, we will be done with the worst of it. Mother's sewing room is always tidy and will only need a dusting and our room, although far from neat, won't need much more."

I heard my mother call up the stairwell, "Fiona, Fiona! I'm sending Kathleen up. The wee whirlwind is under-foot and Meg, Molly and I can't get a thing done!"

I, being the oldest Gearaghty girl, was considered second in command in caring for the younger children, which I must admit, I lorded over my good-natured little Chloe, but found it to be a real thorn in my side sometimes when dealing with four-year-old Kathleen, commonly known as Katy. A sound of little footsteps preceded my babe sister's boisterous entrance, her golden curls bobbing about and a smear of breakfast jam on her chubby cheeks.

"Fi! Fi! Mam says I can help you. Mam says you HAVE to let me help!"

"All right! All right! Calm yerself down and let me find something you can do. Ah! I know just the thing. "

"Chloe," I asked, "Would you give her some of those dust rags and put her to task on the chests?"

With Katy now happy and occupied, Chloe took the bed linens down to be aired. I then focused on sweeping up as much of the fine dust as possible so when I mopped it wouldn't create a muddy mess.

"Fi! Me rags is all dirty now. I want clean ones." demanded Katy

"I don't have more. Just shake them out the window and don't drop them. I don't have time to go all the way downstairs to the yard to get them," I warned her.

A few moments later, I happened to turn toward the window and my eyes went wide. Time seemed to slow to a crawl as I realized Katy had moved the step stool from the high bedside over to the window. She was now standing on the stool, balanced on her tiny toes, leaning forward and vigorously shaking the rags. Without conscious thought, I realized her body was tipping forward and would be past the point of no return in mere seconds. In two long steps, I reached Katy and grabbed the back of her smock just as she started to fall. She let out a banshee yell and all I can recall seeing were two bare, kicking, feet with grubby soles and a rosy white bottom as her smock fell forward over her head. I quickly hauled her in, praying she didn't slip through the wide neck of her shift before I could get her to safety. By the time the little one was inside, and in my arms, my heart was beating so hard I was sure it would burst. A quick look at Katy's face also warned me she was on the verge of letting loose another ear-splitting wail.

Self-preservation kicked in and muffling her a bit against my shoulder, I softly said,

"Whisht, whisht, Katy. It's all right. You're fine now. Don't cry, don't cry. Mam will hear, and she might be angry and not let you go with me to the pasture to put Lamby in the shed. This will be our little secret, aye?"

I knew, of course, I was the one who would be in serious trouble if Mother had any idea how closely a tragedy was averted. A picture suddenly formed of what it would be like should our family have to bury another child next to little Aileen in the cemetery. I knew how devastated we all were, but especially my parents, when Aileen was taken by the fever before she ever saw her first birthday. I could never forgive myself should I ever be the cause for such grief.

Even though Katy was still snuffling like a little piglet, my admonishment had the desired effect and she calmed down. I, on the other hand, was shaking like a palsied old woman. Making sure to tell Katy to stay away from the window and to let me do the shaking of the rags, any previous daydreaming and procrastination suddenly disappeared. Chloe returned from hanging out the bedding to find me hard at work, a serious and determined taskmaster. She had no idea why this change had taken place, but she knew immediately it would not be in her best interests to question me.

By early evening the upstairs was cleaned to mother's satisfaction and the household returned to its normal routine. Father would be home soon, and we could all tell by the delightful aromas from the kitchen that we would have one of Meg's wonderful fish stews, heavy with cream and shiny with melted butter floating on the top. It would be filled with mussels, delicate white fish and any other surprises she was able to get today at the fishmongers. This was always served with heavy oat bread and the rich butter for which County Corke was famous.

Father, a successful wine merchant, was also on the Town Council and was sure to come home with the latest happenings, rumors, and rumors of rumors. As a man of his stature, he was also expected to do his fair share of entertaining. This was no chore for him because he knew as much business as might be accomplished at the Government house during the day, even more was learned and put into action over a decanter of fine Portugues port and a satisfying meal.

In fact, I knew he was having one such supper the next evening for I heard Mother ask Meg if her cousin Bridie was coming the next morning as planned. Bridie was bossy and brusque and had little patience with children, which surprised me as she had twelve of her own. Come to think of it, this might explain her attitude! She was also large and buxom, and Chloe and I secretly called her 'Senora Santa Domingo' because her prow was massive and rode before her like a Spanish galleon coming into port. However, she was a wonder of a cook. She could take a scrawny duck, last year's apples, and a handful of oat flour and make a meal fit for a king! Whenever she arrived, we all turned the kitchen over to her and merely stood ready to fulfill her commands, even mother.

While waiting for Da to come home, I thought I would fulfill my promise to Katy and take her up the hill in back to put our sheep, Lamby, up for the night. She had long outgrown the cute name we had given her, for she was fully grown with her wool getting long and shaggy in preparation for the winter ahead. I found Katy building a little doll's house with some kindling.

"Do ye want to come with me to the pasture Katy?"

Her face lit up and she was at my side in a quick moment.

"Get your shawl, darlin'. It's blowing an unusually cold breeze out back."

Hand in hand, we opened the back gate dividing the walled kitchen garden from the rich grasses on the uphill slope of pasture. I could see Lamby not too far from the stone shed where we locked her in at night. Not only was the shed warmer for her, it was protection from men and beasts roaming after dark which might like to make a fine meal out of her.

Just to the other side of the shed was the Faerie Tree. Many pastures around had such hawthorn trees for they were thought to be the domain of the Faeries. They were left in place when the fields were cleared as it was said ill fortune would befall anyone foolish enough to damage or cut down a Faerie Tree. Some had been around for so long, and were so readily accessible to all, that they were thick with colorful cloughties tied upon their branches. These rags were tied by the dreamers and the hopeful as a prayer, or omen, to the spirits of the Faeries. This was one of my favorite spots to sit and dream in the summer sun and I had a fair share of me own cloughties on the tree.

Katy spotted the sheep and called out. "Lamby! Come girl, I have a wee treat for you from the kitchen."

She didn't have to call twice. The ewe lifted her head from feeding and when her soft brown eyes spotted us, down the hill she came.

Our cozy little shed had plenty of room to allow for the babies Lamby foaled in the spring and a low, but good, sod roof to keep it dry. Rain drained off into a stone trough to provide water for the ewe and there was a separate side area laid with thrushes for the few bits of equipment we needed. It had some thick branches laid across the opening between the storage area and the sheep's keep. This was to prevent Lamby from getting into the fodder laid aside for when it would be needed. Once she was settled in, had eaten greens Katy brought, and got enough snuggles from us, we headed back, closing the sturdy wooden door behind us. Da should be home by now and relaxing in the library. It was a good time to have a few moments with him.

He was sitting in front of a small turf fire already laid against the unseasonal coolness of the evening and didn't see me yet as he was concentrating on some documents. For all his importance, he was simply my dear Da to me. The head of rich chestnut hair my mother described had now turned quite grey and wasn't so thick. Time had left its mark on his strong face, but his blue eyes were the same. They were warm, intelligent, kind and sparkled often with his humor. He seldom lost patience with his family, although rumor had it, he was a firm man with his employees and not likely to suffer fools in politics or business.

"Da, welcome home! May I have a moment?"

He looked up and instantly gave me a big smile.

"Of course, Darlin'. Come sit," he said patting the footstool in front of him.

"Mam says we're having company tomorrow. Who is coming?"

"A few of our councilmen, Roland Fitzpatrick and, of course, my clerk, Thomas Lydon. It seems there have been very believable rumors of an Armada of Spaniards on its way to Ireland to join some of our Chieftains against the English. We can be sure Queen Elizabeth knows about this, but where they are planning to land is pure conjecture. It should be a lively supper conversation, no?"

Quite taken aback, I asked, "Do you think Kinsale is in any danger? It's not like we're a threat to the English!"

"It's the very thing we need to discuss," he explained, "There's only a small British garrison here and they give us little trouble. We're allowed to practice our Catholic faith and they don't interfere with our trade, even with France and Spain. It may all come to naught like the Armada in the late 1500's, not that I would wish such destruction and loss of life on any venture."

I was relieved and agreed as I couldn't see Kinsale as anything more than the quiet, safe and prosperous village I had always known. I stood and gave him a hug and said I was sure they would know how to handle it. I took my leave to contemplate issues which were more personal and imminent.

For one, I wasn't surprised he had invited Roland Fitzpatrick. Not only was he related to the Earl of Desmond, just to the north of us, but also to the Galway Lynch's, successful merchants and leaders in their own right. Roland was ambitious and his two main goals were to grow his own trade in butter and hides and to partner with Father's very lucrative wine trade. Both he and father also wanted to expand the kelp trade. The large quantity of seaweed in our area was highly valued as a fertilizer throughout the rocky farms in Ireland and the inland areas of Europe. Roland had also let my father know he would like my hand in marriage. Such a match with me would go a long way in him achieving both of his other goals.

Father had already discussed this with me to see if I had any interest in such a match. Although it was customary in Ireland for girls to marry in their late teens, and for them to have a preference in their choice of husbands, the father was still the patriarch and had the final say. Therefore, I was much pleased father was giving me a choice. Of course, it was a good match; Roland was a handsome man and only about 10 years older than me, of a good family and had taken his inheritance and name and become quite well off, if not wealthy.

I admitted to my father I wasn't sure I was ready to be wed, nor did I want to make such a promise so soon. Father smiled, took my hands and said,

"Since you're not yet seventeen and there bein' no need to rush on any account, I see no reason for Fitzpatrick to expect an immediate commitment. Besides, I know the man is hungry to join our business ventures together. He has good reason to force himself to be patient, so I believe the 'dog will wait for his bone'!"

I wasn't quite pleased to be referred to as 'a bone', but I understood what Father was saying. However, I did have some other personal qualms about not accepting the offer right away. A friend of mine, Sinead, had turned down a perfectly acceptable suitor when about my age and the gentleman took the hand of another within six months. When she couldn't decide on another, her father finally lost patience and arranged for her to marry a wealthy, but an altogether homely man a good thirty years older. The Gearaghty family attended the wedding where the groom spent most of the ceremony leering at his young bride and Sinead wept through the whole service. I prayed to all the Saints that such a fate never befalls me.

In fact, I brought my fears to my mother one night and said perhaps it would be a mistake to not accept Roland's offer although I felt much too young to become the lady of his household, not to mention broaching the subject of fulfilling my duties in the bedchamber. My mother smiled knowingly and drew me to her breast, much as she had when comforting me as a child.

"Now, Fiona, you mustn't fret. I happen to know you have been blessed with those qualities which attract a man. You have a crown of shimmering caramel-colored hair that is naturally thick and wavy; you have a fine figure which is a delight to behold and eyes as clear and blue as the sea on a summer's day. Better yet, you are a warm and loving person, although still a bit rebellious for my liking, "she teased, "I don't say this just because you're mine. I say this because you look much like me at your age and by the time, I was two years older than you are now, I had several fine suitors from which to choose. However, Francis Gearaghty was the one I wanted, and it turned out to be a good decision. He is a kind and considerate husband and an excellent father."

I knew this to be true for I had seen the warmth and respect my parents had for each other. They showed no shame in often sharing a quick, but warm kiss and I had caught my father, on occasion, giving mother a little pat on her bum.

As usual, Mother had said the right thing. My worries dissolved like a mist and my natural optimism returned.

Not too long after this discussion about Roland's earlier offer, I was called to Father's library. He told me he was not entirely surprised, but his clerk, Thomas Lydon, had hinted he would like to put himself forward as a suitor for my hand. My eyes grew wide and even though my mouth opened, nothing came forth.

"Well girl, surely you have something to say. It's not like you could have missed his interest in you. Do you really think he has spent so much time at our home because he's enamored of clerking for me?"

"But, uh, Father," I stammered, "This can't be true. I've known Thomas all my life. He's like a brother to me. We are, or have been, playmates. Of course, I'm very fond of him and I think him a very upright and decent man. But do you think he's a good suitor? Why, he doesn't even have a proper home!"

"Those are the very points we discussed Fiona and I also apprised him of Fitzpatrick's offer. I was honest and told him you had not, as yet, accepted. I am also very aware he is not socially an appropriate suitor, but something tells me he will do well in the world, whether he stays with me, or embraces other opportunities. Fitzpatrick, on the other hand, has not been subtle in pointing out marrying you would be a step down. I have no doubt he would remind you of it at times, should it be to his advantage to do so. However, Thomas, being a gentleman, and caring for your welfare, despite his heart's desire, saw the truth of it. I only tell you this so you know the way of things and so you don't inadvertently give him false hope."

I assured Father I wasn't planning on doing so, but I must admit, this news gave me much to ponder later. I now couldn't help but see him in different light. I had always found him most pleasing to look upon. He was one of those rare southern coast Irish blessed with blue-black hair, chocolate brown eyes and a light complexion with high color. Although not overly tall, he was nicely built with a slim waist and still several inches taller than I. One of the reasons we had been such fast friends is because, even though he was educated, especially in languages and mathematics, he never talked down to me. We would have wonderful conversations and he went out of his way to become my unofficial tutor and taught me to read and write. On the other hand, there really was the issue regarding his not having a home, for he slept in a loft room above St. Multose Church in trade for keeping church records of births, deaths and marriages. He had a most beautiful and readable script which, besides his work for Father and a room at the church, gave him some additional income by those who required legible written documents. Even though he would probably make a more companionable mate, I finally made up my mind we were friends and must stay thus. After all, a woman had to consider her security and status first!

CONVERSATIONS AND CONCERNS – KINSALE

The next day dawned bright and clear with freshening breezes from the coast. This was welcome at the end of August as the weather could either be grand, or a nasty reminder of winter coming early! I was awakened by noises which let me know the staff was already a bustle in preparation for guests that evening. I knew we would be in for a light breakfast of breads and beer. I was hoping we would also get a plate of stewed apples with cinnamon. Da was fortunate to get a shipment of such a special spice occasionally which would go a long way toward improving our winter fare. Months of pickled, dried and salted foods could become quite tiresome. This reminded me that I must remember to give thanks in my morning prayers for the weather and the food, for there would be many in Ireland this winter who would have little enough to eat. We had heard the stories of armed forces leaving farms and crops burnt to the ground in their wake, without a thought to the survival of farmers and their families. It was shameful to hear these troops were not just those of Queen Elizabeth in her quest to conquer and colonize my country, but the same deeds were done by the followers of the Chieftains as they also tried to deny the English troops sustenance from the land.

Well, I decided, I best get out of bed and get involved in the day's activities to put my mind in a better place. I noted Chloe and Katy were already up and out. I could just see dear Chloe taking tousle headed Katy in tow to keep her from waking me. Chloe was so kindhearted. I wished I could be more like her.

All was humming smoothly when we were surprised to see father home almost an hour before his usual time. He greeted us warmly and checked with mother to ensure all was going as planned. However, he seemed distracted. I asked him if he would like some beer and cake. He simply gave me a, "Hrmmph.", which I took as a yes. He then went into the library and closed the door behind him. A bit later I knocked and entered. Setting the beer and plate down I asked him, "Is all well Da? You seem distraught."

He looked at me blankly for a moment then blinked as though coming back from far away.

"Oh! Not to worry Fiona. We've heard additional rumors regarding the Spaniard's ships floating about which needs verification. I am glad I planned this evening together as these concerns need to be discussed. Put it aside for now dear. I'm sure it's nothing."

His furrowed brow belied his words, but I felt it best to leave him to ponder in private and I let myself out of the room.

It was only a short time later when there was a knock at the front door. Since Meg and all were busy, I answered and saw Thomas standing there. Surprised at his early arrival, I noted his wavy hair was mussed, which usually indicated some worry because of his habit of running his fingers through it when dealing with problems. Somewhat flustered by my being the one to answer the door, he stammered a greeting and said he had to see father right off. I noticed he was clutching his ever-present satchel and a fistful of documents. I directed him to the library where he scurried in and closeted himself with father.

Mother came in. "What's going on? I thought I heard Thomas."

"You did," I answered. "I don't know what's going on, but it must be either government concerns or about father's business. I can't hear what they are saying, but it sounds serious. We may learn about some interesting goings on tonight, aye?"

"Well, no matter what Fiona, you girls better get upstairs and get changed or our guests will catch you all in your shifts! I'll have Molly come up and do your hair. She's wonderful at putting' your hair up with those braids which make it look like you're wearing a crown."

Roland Fitzpatrick arrived late, as was his custom, which was no problem as my clever mother knew she could assume he would. He looked quite elegant in his brown velvet doublet with embroidery on the sleeves. He wore a fashionable white ruff, but it was a bit large, in the English fashion. This struck me as somewhat ostentatious for an informal supper in Kinsale! He unbuckled his sword, removed his cape with a rather theatrical flourish, and dropped them into Meg's waiting arms. Mam looked lovely in her pearl pendant and rose-colored gown. The hue put a bloom in her cheeks and the white starting to appear in her hair simply appeared as silver lights woven in the gold. She would now be considered a handsome woman, but the beauty of her youth was still quite apparent.

Roland came sauntering over to her, bowed courteously and said, "I look forward to a lovely evening Mistress Gearaghty" as he kissed her hand. He then complimented me and placed his lips upon my hand, but with a little less ardor than I would have expected. By then Da and Thomas joined us. Roland greeted Father with a bow and congratulated him on the safe arrival of his favorite ship and cargo of wine from Bordeaux. He merely nodded to Thomas.

The room was soon filled with chatter and the clinking of glasses. I saw Mother give a signal to Molly and we were quickly joined by wee Katy who had been properly instructed on how to wish us all a good evening before she went upstairs for her supper and to be tucked into bed. I remembered my mother doing the same for me at her age and how very grown up I felt to be included.

"I again apologize for arriving early," said Thomas as he came to stand by my side. "I must tell you; you look lovely this evening Fiona Your green gown compliments your hair perfectly. In fact, I saw a lady today wearing an emerald necklace which would have been stunning on you."

He automatically glanced down at my bosom to envisage the necklace and quickly averted his eyes and turned quite pink. Looking up, he gave me a warm smile and a soft touch on my arm before moving on to speak to mother. Even as a boy, just a few years older than I, he never teased me as the other lads did. He seemed to have a natural ability to be kind and had an uncanny awareness of other's feelings.

While waiting for supper to be served, I glanced over and saw Da, Roland and Thomas standing side by side with another group of gentlemen. The first thing I noticed was, even though father was getting a bit greyer and a tad portlier, he cut a very prosperous figure in his conservative, yet quality, clothing. The long overcoat of burgundy cut off at just the right length to let his dark blue hose accent his still sturdy calves.

Roland was tall and fair haired. I noticed he had recently shaped his beard, so it only covered his chin and was tapered to a point. It was attractive as it lengthened his face. However, I became aware it also revealed a somewhat receding chin line. How had I not noticed before? He used his hands a lot in conversation which was not a drawback since he had long tapered fingers and the nails were neatly kept.

I noted Thomas, though taller than I, was still an inch or so shorter than Roland. I grinned as I saw he was running his fingers through his hair again as he got caught up in the conversation. He had always done this, yet his hair had such a natural wave to it, even though it might look a bit untidy, it never looked bedraggled. His hands were also well cared for, but his fingertips were permanently stained with the marks of his trade. His clothing was, of course, of less quality, but well cared for. I spotted several areas on his hose which had been mended but mended well and the flat collar was clean and white. It pleased me to see he was wearing the collar on which I had embroidered a subtle Celtic design in the corners as a birthday gift to him. All and all, a nice group of men in my life, I thought.

The ongoing conversations continued as we were served supper. However, I was aware, as the evening wore on, Father and Thomas were growing more tense.

Toward the end of the meal, Da stood and tapped the edge of his goblet for attention.

"My dear friends. You were originally invited this evening simply to break bread with us and enjoy each other's company. However, there have been some developments, of which you should be made aware before the rumor mill runs amok. We have just received some dispatches from Corke verifying stories of a Spanish Armada again rallying against Elizabeth's forces."

"That's ridiculous!" interrupted one of the Councilmen. "The last Armada years ago didn't fare very well for the Spaniards, as we all know."

"Yes! This is why we are in such a quandary. It's my understanding they only set sail less than a week ago and the English undoubtedly wouldn't have missed the bustle and preparations on the west coast of Portugal, so their sailing is no secret. At this point no one seems to know exactly where they plan to land, but we do think we know why. As you know, the English have conquered and colonized the majority of Ireland. We are required to abide by English rules and, as much as they would like us to embrace their culture and religion, they do allow us much leeway. However, in Ulster in the North, it is a different story. Hugh O'Neill, Earl of Tyrone, has been playing cat and mouse with Queen Elizabeth for years. He has his clans submit to her and then he is in her favor. However, intermittently, he decides he wants Ireland for the Irish, gets some of the northern clans to back him and creates skirmishes with the English troops."

"What has it to do with us?" asked Roland. "The Queen's representatives in Dublin and Corke have no dispute with our trade. After all, they do quite well on taxes and levies as our ships leave from or off-load at Corke. Let the Spanish and English continue their conflict. The more we can keep them embroiled in our north, the less likely they are to interfere with our prosperity in the south!"

A few "Hear, hears" were heard around the table.

"I must admit, the merchant in me and the politician in me, hear what you are saying," Father said. "However, the Irish in me balks at refusing our chieftains the right to fight for what is ours. Thomas has obtained some documents, or copies thereof, which may give us a different opinion on O'Neill's ultimate intent. Thomas, would you be good enough to share this information?"

"Of course," said Thomas, standing. "Some of you may have heard a rumor to this effect, but now I have a verification that in September of '95 O'Neill, one of our most powerful Irish Lords and some of his supporters in Ulster wrote to the King of Spain soliciting aid. He asserted the only hope of reestablishing the Catholic religion throughout Ireland lay with help from Spain's Philip III. O'Neill officially broke with the English crown in February of '95. In '98, with his son-in-law Red Hugh O'Donnell, who despises the English, as a flea hates water, raided a resupply force coming from Armagh to the Crown's Blackwater Fort. It was a rout and Elizabeth has not forgotten the insult! Such victories in the north encouraged O'Neill to promise King Phillip that with two or three thousand Spanish troops he and his supporters hoped to restore the faith of the church and secure the Spanish King a new kingdom. We also have other documents he wrote restating he felt, with the aid of these extra troops, the Catholic faith in Ireland might be re-established and within one year, the heretics would disappear, and no other sovereign would be recognized save Philip as our Catholic King."

Councilman O'Rourke half rose from his seat and blustered, "You mean to say they are

planning on an island-wide war to oust Elizabeth and then to hand our country over to another foreign ruler? The only benefit I can see to such a plan is the Catholic religion would be the official, dominant religion for the Irish."

"The point is," responded Father," what O'Neill and the King of Spain see in such an endeavor is to re-establish Ireland for the Irish as well ingratiating themselves to His Holiness, the Pope. O'Neill will undoubtedly plan to make some arrangements with Philip which would leave O'Neill very much in charge, somewhat as an emissary, or de facto, ruler of Ireland. There is also one more incentive for the Spaniards to fight for us," he interjected." Once they have helped us win our freedom and the reunification of Ireland, they gain a stronger hold on the seas and have an excellent and easier foothold from which to conduct trade, conquer England and enthrone a Catholic ruler there. This is an excellent time to make such a move with the Queen's health declining. It is likely a new monarch will be needed in England soon anyway."

"Well, God's blood! O'Neill's letter of appeal was made about six years ago. Why are we only seeing a Spanish force now?" queried Roland.

Father leaned forward and said," I have given this some thought too. It appears Philip has sporadically sent a few troops, arms and a little money. However, it is quite well known he strains the treasury of Spain with frivolous and extravagant spending. Wars are costly, and we must assume he has been unable to put together a force to support the Irish until now. Regarding where they plan to land, I think the best guess is the Spanish will make their way up the west coast to Limerick, or preferably Galway, in order to meet up with the Irish chieftain's northern forces.

Well Gentlemen, I think it's time for us to withdraw to the library and discuss what will be best for the security of our town and families, depending on where the Spaniards land. "

Roland stood looking around the table, then boldly at me, and stated, "Let me be the first to

swear, should any fighting, or battles, ensue in Kinsale, I shall join in the fight against the English and protect the citizens of this town. I shall defend the defenseless!"

The men then withdrew, and mother had Chloe and me stay at the table for she knew we also had some decisions to make.

" Girls, what I believe to be true is," explained mother," no matter what happens with this Spanish Armada, unless of course they are destroyed at sea as the last one, it is going to make a difference in our lives. The only unknown is whether it will affect us sooner, rather than later. No matter where they land, there will be no way of avoiding thousands of men living off our land and ensuing battles disrupting transportation and trade of foodstuffs."

I glanced over at Chloe and saw her eyes wide and a slight tremble to her lower lip. I put my arms around her little shoulders, as much to comfort myself as to comfort her. I asked mother what we could possibly do to avoid this.

"First of all, I need to speak with your father to get himself and the other merchants to bring in as many supplies as possible, as quickly as possible. Right now, the seas seem open, but it could change quickly. Then we, as should all of those in Kinsale, start to harvest whatever crops remain in the gardens and fields and start preserving them and then do the same with any new food supplies we get. I will also suggest people create places to store much of the food in a way which will not be so obvious to any friend or foe choosing to spend time in Kinsale.

Whether they are the English, Spanish, or Irish forces, feeding themselves first will be their main concern. The town councilmen will know how to stress the wisdom of taking these precautions. Now we must pray and get to work. I will explain what is going on to Meg and Molly as they will see their workload increase too."

It was as Mother said. Our days were busy and the winding, narrow streets of Kinsale bustled with activity as new shipments of grains, ale, vegetables and salted meat were delivered. When I went to town, the stone basins near the fishmongers, were crowded with women cleaning and salting the fresh fish as fast as they could. I had to admit, I found it quite exciting to walk about the town and sense the single mindedness. The air also was filled with the scents of fall and a definite drop in temperature. Even during the warmest days of summer women often wore their shawls as the meandering narrow streets, tiers of houses on the hillsides and tightly clustered buildings prevented the penetration of much sunshine in the center of Kinsale.

I also noticed more nervousness and tension in the English troops attached to the small garrison posted here. Their commander, William Saxey, was no doubt hoping to be in defense of a town which would not come under attack. However, it was observed he was frequenting the drinking establishments a bit more often than usual. Most of his command was stationed at the fortifications of Ringcurran and Castle Ni Park, for those would be the first line of defense, should a force attempt to enter the harbour

By mid-September, the unused fourth room upstairs, was stocked with non-edibles, like linens, tallow and crockery, which we moved up from the cellar to make more room for foodstuffs. We then had a false wall created in the cellar. This space was designated to hide preserved foods, the good wines and medicinal herbs. Enough was stacked in front of it to satisfy others who might make demands upon our personal supplies to assume what they saw was all we had. We also understood and accepted meals would be more meagre than usual, but there were no complaints for we were well aware of the possible repercussions of excess.

Father received reports from our transports that there had been some rough seas between Spain and Ireland, but no verifiable knowledge of the status, or location of this armada. When the council heard this, they decided if the Spanish couldn't get as far as Galway or Limerick, they would probably aim for Corke. It was only eighteen miles to the east of us, but was under tight control of the

English, so one could assume there would be fierce fighting which would keep both sides busy. Roland, Father and most other merchants decided to reroute any shipping away from the harbour at Corke until we knew where the battles would take place. As it turned out, their guess regarding Corke was right, and wrong!

SEPTEMBER 22, 1601 – KINSALE

I was restless and unable to sleep well. I finally gave up and arose early. Dressed and prepared for a typical day, I sensed a change in the usual noises outside. Voices we wouldn't normally hear this far from town, or the quay, could be heard, loud and strident. My mouth dropped open as I looked from the upstairs window toward the south. The estuary and harbour were filling with ships, most carrying the flags of Spain, of all sizes and many had appeared to have been damaged in rough weather. We could hear echoes of what seemed to be cannon fire and saw smoke near the Castle Ni Park fort where the English garrison was on guard. It was obvious the armada we assumed would bypass us, had not!

Father had already left for town, so the rest of us grabbed our shawls and cloaks and with Colum carrying Katy, we flew down the steep hill, too breathless to even venture guesses about how and in what way this phenomenal event would affect to us.

By the time we got to the quay, some ships were already off-loading men in armor and weaponry, which led us to believe the confrontation at the forts was not going well for the English for there seemed to be little concern about further protecting the ships in the harbour.

My heart was beating hard and not just from the run down the hill. Even though I knew the Spanish were at war with England and they were allegedly here at The

O'Neill's request, it was rather frightening to see so many soldiers gathered in Kinsale. I could also sense I wasn't the only one with those concerns. There was a palpable tension in the crowd even as some onlookers cheered.

It appeared like a scene at a mad house. Men were shouting in Spanish, Italian, Portuguese, even Irish and Scots. Women were trying to control their crying, frightened children and the Priests seemed to be intent on very loud prayers, blessings and preaching.

As we backed away, making room for the crowds and for the soldiers to be brought forward, we saw the main gate to the city opened wide and the mayor and council, including Father, coming forward. They met briefly with a slight man in rather ornate armor and colorful clothing. His demeanor made it clear he was in charge. The Mayor and entourage gave him a slight bow and walked back to wait at the main gate.

The commander mustered his troops in some sort of marching order, but I couldn't take my eyes off the continual off-loading of more persons. There were priests, nuns, women and children by the score. This seemed strange to the extreme in what should be a military force. By the time the armed troops, under twenty-five colorful banners, were set to march toward the town, there had to have been over three thousand persons landed. This almost doubled the size of our town's population.

I suspected our walled city contained no more than two-hundred proper houses and could not fathom how we could house and support this huge mass of, what? Were they invaders, allies, usurpers? It was quite worrisome. Since we were docile and cooperative with the English, would we now be in danger? Will the Spaniards take over Kinsale, putting us once again under another military rule, thereby making us enemies of both England and the Irish Lords?

Before entering the town, the commander marched his troops up and down making quite a show of strength. He then spoke at length again with the Mayor and counsel. They seemed to come to an agreement, whereby the Spanish commander stood upon the high ground at the gate and looking down over the gathered citizens proclaimed,

" **We, Don Juan de Aguila, general of the army to Phillip III, King of Spain, by these presents, does promise that all the inhabitants of the town of Kinsale shall receive no injury by any of our retinue, but rather shall be used as our brethren and friends, and that it shall be lawful for any of the inhabitants that list to transport, without any molestation in body or goods, and as much as shall remain, likewise without any hurt.**"

He basically told us we could leave, if we wanted to, without harm, or stay, as we wished. I could almost hear a collective sigh of relief and lightening of spirit from the crowd. I looked at mother and could detect a relaxation in her face. The Sovereign Mayor of Kinsale, ceremonial rod in hand, proudly escorted Aguila and his entourage into the town. The Armada had landed.

Aguila spent the next few days transferring most of his forces and the sundry mix of others, in and around the two fortifications at the mouth of the harbour. The English troops there had wasted little time in abandoning their posts and heading toward Corke to report and join any forces there.

The Mayor established the Spanish headquarters in town at Desmond Castle. This one-hundred-year old square castle was not chosen for its comfort. It was cold, damp, poorly laid out and drafty and was positioned on a steep hillside above the quay. However, what Aguila saw was a sweeping view of the harbour, a defensible structure should the town's walls be breached plus high ground from which to defend against an assault. Unfortunately, to impress our new 'guests', the mayor also commandeered quite a few private homes to host some of the higher ranked militia. Since we didn't want their presence here anyway, this did not sit well with many of the townspeople.

As soon as the Commander was settled, he began meetings and consultations with the Town Counsel and his staff. There was a steady stream in and out of his headquarters perched above us. I must admit, it was comical to see our Mayor, who was less than fit, huffing and puffing up the castle's hill, ceremonial rod in hand, several times a day!

Father kept us apprised as word reached us from Corke and Dublin. The English were as surprised as we regarding the Spanish landing in Kinsale. The armada's ships had been pummeled by storms, many of them tossed about and separated from the main force. They attempted to find refuge in Corke harbour as Da thought they might. But just as they started limping toward its entrance, a strong head wind came up which pushed them back out to sea and gave them no choice but to head for

Kinsale. Less than half of the more than fifty ships which left Portugal found safety in our harbour and they were now about as far away from the promised Irish forces in the north as they could be.

Father invited Aguila to our home for an informal discussion of the situation at hand. It wasn't difficult to entice him with a promise of warm comfort, decent food and wine. It seems he and Da had taken a liking to each other. Aguila was a brusque, but honest, warrior and father found him to be quick and intelligent. They both felt it was to their advantage to discuss all their options, for the good of the town and the Spanish forces. The family, the Mayor, Thomas and Roland were all there by the time Aguila and his Aide de Camp arrived. I was quite excited to see Aguila up close. He wasn't overly tall, but his attitude and bearing left no doubt he was a man of action. I was also surprised he wasn't heavy, for most military men I saw who had reached a certain age and rank, had a tendency toward overweight. His hair was trimmed short and neat as was his beard and mustache. This was a man who gave me confidence. He was introduced around and then he introduced the Spaniard with him. "This is Rodrigo Lopez de Avila, my Aide de Camp."

de Avila was lean and taller than his commander and might be considered attractive but for an excessive sharpness to his features. His luxurious head of loose black curls and light olive complexion gave him an exotic look and I was quite fascinated by the single tear drop pearl dangling from his ear. I hadn't seen this fashion before, but it did create a feminine counter point to his obvious masculinity! His manners were as one would expect from a man of good family. He bowed deeply to the Mayor, my father, Roland and Thomas, He took my mother's hand and kissed it as he did mine. However, I felt his lips linger overlong and there was a definite hint of sensuousness as his hand slipped from mine. In surprise, I glanced at him and saw a subtle smirk at getting away with this impropriety. It was all I could do to keep from wiping the back of my hand on my dress. I believe Roland also noticed as his brow was furrowed watching this scene. I tried to converse with the Spaniard, to be polite, but it was obvious he spoke little English. I finally gave up since my attempts only seemed to give him an excuse to look at me and, more often than not, his eyes were lingering on my bosom. I simply shifted my attention to Chloe and Mother.

Once the niceties were observed, the gentlemen got down to business. I was pleased when they settled to talk in the library with the doors open for, I would be able to hear the conversation while going about my business. Meg and Molly were busy in the kitchen, so my help was not needed there.

"Are you fairly well settled in at the Castle, Commander?" asked Father.

"Si, si. It is an advantageous position and is roomy enough for my needs at this time or should there be a siege. I have lived under much harsher conditions, I assure you!" he smiled. "My concerns are many though. Even though I had planned on landing much further north and with a much larger force, I still assumed the Irish forces promised would have been close enough to join me. I have sent word to O'Neill of Tyrone and Hugh O'Donnell that I have arrived, and an explanation of my situation here. I have had no word and only rumors they are still in, or near the north. I am also waiting for word from the two Irish leaders here in the south, a Florence

MacCarthy and James FitzThomas Fitzgerald." Turning to the Mayor, he asked, "Where are they?"

The mayor looked flustered; his glances darting around the room. "I thought you knew! They have both been arrested and are, by now, locked up in the Tower of London."

Aguila exploded with what was obviously a Spanish expletive!

"I have been thwarted by the weather, mislead by my King and betrayed by my Irish allies. I have with me hundreds of saddles and no horses to put under them! I have large cannons, but no animals to haul them. I have copious quantities of salt and little meat available on which to use it. I am in defense of a fortified town whose walls were built to withstand catapults and arrows, not cannon fire. Commanders cannot fight with unfulfilled promises and my ships, half of which never arrived, are in no condition to go north in hopes of meeting up with Irish forces."

There was silence in the room. The others had nothing to say which would change any of those facts. This was certainly not the appropriate time to complain that Kinsale would also suffer due to Aguila's forces consuming Kinsale's meagre winter supplies. The men did finally reassure the Commander they would do their best to find out the whereabouts of O'Neill and the latest news on the English troops.

Father wisely suggested this was a good time for all take advantage of the last of the late summer sunlight and continue their discussion in a more congenial tone by taking a walk in the gardens. Mother and I joined them. It was good to get out of the house and enjoy the bit of green and colors which were still left before the barrenness of winter arrived. There was a pleasant contrast between the brackish scent of the sea and the aromatic herbs along the path.

As we walked, something caught my eye at the base of the birdbath. Upon investigation, I found a wee bird trying desperately to fly. My exclamation of distress caught the attention of the others and Thomas hurried over to see what was wrong. He picked the bird up gently and we sat on a bench. Roland glanced over and proclaimed the bird had obviously broken its wing and should be abandoned, or if one cared to waste their time, put out of its misery.

Thomas said nothing but continued to examine the bird.

"Ah ha!" he suddenly exclaimed.
The pitiful thing has a thorn under its wing."

I then saw a very tiny branch under the portion of the wing closest to its body and on it was a thorn which penetrated the flesh. Thomas gently pulled it loose and laid the bird back on the ground. After a couple of attempts, the bird realized it could move its wing freely, without pain and took flight. I was so delighted I hugged Thomas as I had when we were children and his face lit up.

Roland simply said "Harrumph!" and rushed to catch up with the other gentlemen.

Thomas and I rose and continued our walk when he noticed I was trembling a bit. The temperature had dropped, and I was feeling the chill. Thomas kindly took off his cloak and draped it over my shoulders. I protested, but he said it was no problem for his clothes without the cape were much warmer than my gown. I thanked him most sincerely as his cloak still radiated his body heat and smelled slightly ink and spice. I recognized the spicy scent as the soap my father imported and was pleased to know he had given some of it to his faithful clerk. We caught up with the group and Roland noticed the cloak.

"You shouldn't have to suffer the cold, Lydon," he admonished. "Fiona should be old enough to realize when an outer wrap might be necessary!"

De Avila also noticed the exchange and said something under his breath. I couldn't understand it, but it was clearly not complimentary. Whether it was directed at me, Thomas or Roland, I knew not. Thomas excused himself, nonchalantly went over to de Avila and whispered something in fluent Spanish to him. De Avila's jaw tightened and his faced flushed red.

Fortunately, Molly happened to choose this moment to announce supper was to be served and we all headed back to the house.

OCTOBER - KINSALE

As fall closed its door on summer, the English Commander, Lord Mountjoy had troops positioned on the hills surrounding Kinsale, but still had no access to the harbour. Aguila was now in hopes, before the English troops in the north could join Mountjoy, he would have some relief with more Spanish ships and the Irish forces would arrive. With the Irish in control above Mountjoy and the Spanish in control of the harbour, the English would be trapped between.

However, Aguila's men didn't simply hide behind Kinsale's walls while they waited. There were skirmishes and raids which caused the English real grief and slowed down their entrenchments. Unfortunately, in walking about the town, it was also easy to see the Spanish troops were underfed and under clothed. There were many men without jackets and even some with no shoes! I don't think the Spanish government realized how the damp winters in Ireland could chill a man to the bones.

Father and his cohorts were also busy from dawn to dusk. Father moved Thomas to our home as having him on hand saved time and I believed he was also concerned about the lack of any heat in Thomas's room in the church loft. It was good to have him at our table for he was an animated and entertaining conversationalist.

I awoke on a mid-October morning hating to leave the warm house to tend to Lamby, but I had to let her out to forage and make sure her water trough wasn't frozen. As I went to get my heavy shawl, I could hear Father and

Thomas in the library and Father's voice was raised in anger.

"Where in God's name is The O'Neill," Da bellowed, "More English forces are joining Mountjoy daily. They must have eight thousand troops now and growing. Our spies have told us they are also bringing more cannons, not that they're trying to hide their capabilities from us! They practically taunt us with them."

"I agree. The Spaniards are doing the best they can, but Aguila has admitted many of his own soldiers are risking being captured by the English, or their own troops, by deserting. They can't help but feel they can scrounge more food and shelter while on the run than by staying here. There have also been reports the English are tormenting O'Donnell's troops as they move south and further delaying the help we need so desperately."

"I know, I know, Da admitted "It would turn the tide if we could get some Irish hounds nipping at Mountjoy's heels. Having them caught in the middle should also discourage those planning on desertion.

Having heard this news, I was giving their conversation much thought as I wrapped myself in my shawl and headed up to the shed. Entering the stone enclosure, I enjoyed the bit of warmth created within by the sheep. Lamby bleated but didn't come toward me. I think she knew I was going to turn her out! As I led her out the door something caught my eye in the side room. Slapping Lamby on the rump, she scampered out and I went back to investigate.

It looked like a messy pile of clothing on the floor. There wasn't much light, so I went into the little side room and I found it to be a bundle tied with rope.

Reaching for the item, I sensed movement behind me and spun around just as a man stepped out of the shadows. I turned quickly toward the door to run away, but he grasped my shawl and pulled me backwards. I opened my mouth to scream and his hand shot out and clamped across my lips. He now had one hand around my waist and my back pressed against him. He removed his hand from my mouth and quickly replaced it with a sharp blade at my throat.

"Silencio" he whispered sharply.

His breath was sour with old wine and he reeked of a man gone too long without bathing. I suddenly realized I knew him. This was Rodrigo de Avila, Aguila's Aide de Camp.

I felt fear turn my blood cold. The bundle at my feet made it clear he was hiding out until he could make his escape from Kinsale. All I could think of was to find a way to get away from him.

"I won't say anything! Just let me go. No one will know!" I promised, not even knowing if he understood what I was saying.

He laughed humorlessly, said something in Spanish and pulled my head back by my hair. He suddenly grasped my bodice, tore it loose and exposed my breasts. I had never felt such helpless fear in my life. With a low growl in his throat, he cruelly grabbed a breast and squeezed so hard I let out a scream. He twisted me around and slapped me hard. My ears rang, and the room tilted.

Throwing me down, he fell upon me. I fought against him, but it was like trying to move a huge stone. I couldn't get any purchase with my bare heels in the slippery dry grass on the floor. Trying to flail around I wasn't sure of exactly what was happening, but was horrified as I knew, without a doubt, he was going to rape me. I started begging him to stop. I told him "No." over and over again.

I felt him fumbling at my skirts and forcing my legs apart with his knee. I finally got one arm loose and swung at him while dragging my nails across his face. He cursed and caught both of my wrists in one hand and held them over my head. I was now no more able to fight than an animal trussed for slaughter. I suddenly felt hot, hard flesh against mine. He clapped his free hand over my mouth again, but before I could even wonder why, I felt a pain like lightening between my legs. I gasped and my eyes flew open. I was staring directly into his face and his eyes were frightening. They were glazed and piercing as he stared at me. Thrusting himself against me; each movement was like a knife going to my deepest core. I could feel my scalding tears run down my face and felt I would be caught in this hell forever.

He suddenly stopped and collapsed on me. I was sobbing and his weight on my chest made me fear I could not breathe. Just when I thought I could get no more air, he arose, rearranged his clothing and laughed. His mouth twisting in a cruel smile, he called me a name which I had no doubt was filthy. Kicking my shawl over me, he grabbed his bundle and left.

I lay there shivering in shock and cold. Rolling over on my side, I curled up like a babe and wept.

As the tears eventually subsided, reality set in and I knew I had to think of what to do.

"Oh, Dear God! I can't tell my parents. What would they think of me? I could never look Da in the face again."

I couldn't even imagine revealing such a thing. Or finding the words to do so. What was the good of it? There was nothing they could do anyway. He was gone, and I was ruined.

"Oh, the shame, the terrible shame of it." is all I could tell myself.

It seemed clear the best decision was to tell not a soul. I would get past it. I would pretend it never happened. The first step now was to get into the house and up to my room before anyone saw me is such a disheveled state. My clothes were torn, my nose had bled, and I could feel a bruise raising on my cheek.

Getting up slowly, I was shocked at the feeling of being bruised all over, which I realized was more the truth of it. I used the icy water in the trough against my battered face and washed away the blood. I pulled my clothes together as best I could, wrapped myself in my shawl and headed back to the house. I hadn't gone more than 10 paces before I was suddenly and violently ill. I wretched until there was nothing left to bring up. The foul taste of my vomit seemed a fitting end to such an attack, yet the purging almost had a sense of cleansing to it.

As I continued toward the house, I realized not much more than an hour could have passed as it was only mid-morning. How could my world have turned upside down in such a short span of time? I no longer felt like me. It was as though the pummeling and violation I suffered had reshaped me.

I entered the kitchen and only Meg noticed my condition.

"Fiona? Are you alright? You've a nasty bruise on your face."

"It's fine Meg. I was running a bit downhill and tripped over a stone. I tumbled headfirst, but it's nothing to fret about. I'll just go to my room and clean up."

To my great relief, she accepted my story with a sympathetic, "Tut-tut." and went back to her kitchen duties.

I escaped upstairs before my mother saw me. I knew she would want more details than I was willing, or able, to give. Entering the familiar surroundings of the bedroom, a feeling of lethargy suddenly came over me. I was simply moving without thought. I automatically took the basin of water with me as I walked behind our privacy screen and slowly rewashed my face. It was so odd. It was as though I was watching myself, but I was not me. I started to undress and vaguely noticed my bodice was not terribly torn, and I simply thought out loud,

"Oh good. I can mend it. I won't have to ask Mother to make a new one."

I removed my skirt, noticing a bloody stain on it and washed it out without any consideration as to how it got there. It was then I noticed the same type of stain and residue on my thighs.

Indifferently, I began to wash myself and abruptly felt a stinging pain in my most private areas. The room instantly grew dark as my vision narrowed and I felt I would be ill again.

I awoke laying on the floor, semi-naked, behind the screen. I don't know how long I was unconscious, but I don't think it was more than a few minutes. I was shaky but was finally able to get dressed.

I didn't know what to do next. I had no one to go to except God. I got on my knees to pray, but I wasn't sure for what I should pray. I knew I didn't do anything to put myself in such a position, yet, we were taught it was a sin to have intimate relations with a man who was not our husband. I was very confused and finally asked God to forgive me if I really had done anything wrong, because I didn't mean to and asked Him to help me keep this terrible secret from my parents.

I stumbled through the rest of the day, clinging desperately to the routines which would anchor me. As the time approached for me to go up the hill and put Lamby back in the shed for the night, I trembled as panic grabbed my heart. I just could not go back there again. What if he was still lurking? Claiming I was not well, I asked my brother Robbie if he would take on the task. One look at my pale face convinced him I truly was ill. Being a kind-hearted young man, he quickly agreed to do so, and I could breathe again. If anyone saw a difference in me, they didn't say anything. This amazed me. I felt my disgrace and humiliation surely surrounded me with a shameful light which all could see.

I awoke the next morning, after a restless night filled with tears and disjointed memories of the attack. I was sore and bruised inside and knew I had to force myself to face this and each following day as any other. I mentally put my secret in a dark little corner of my mind and kept it separate from my real world. Unfortunately, it still festered under the surface like a thorn dug too deep to remove. I was irritable and, for the first time in my life, afraid. One day, Chloe and I went together to do some shopping. While selecting some vegetables, I turned from the farmer's stall to find Chloe gone. I was overwhelmed with panic. My eyes, darting around madly, finally found her over by the fountain, in animated conversation with Mick, the chandler's son.

I reached them in moments and grabbing Chloe roughly, I spoke in anger, "Stay away from my sister you mongrel! She's not yours to entice."

His face registered shock. "We were just talkin' Fiona. I would never do such a thing."

Without a word, I pulled Chloe with me as I hurried away. She was crying. Even though I told her I was just trying to protect her, I also knew, in my heart, to accuse this twelve-year-old boy, who had always been nothing but decent, was wrong and unfair,

Shortly after All Saints Day, I was working in the sewing room and the realization struck me. I had not had my courses this month. They had been as regular as the sunrise from the time I first started. I quickly did some calculations but could not deny I was most assuredly overdue.

"It may just be the shock after what happened," I reassured myself, "this has upset my body's rhythms and I'm sure I will start today, or tomorrow."

However, in my heart, I feared I was wrong. It was very possible I was going to have a child. My dark secret not only reemerged from its hiding place; it had grown a hideous head of destruction. Tears of fear and desolation fell upon my sewing. I didn't know what to do, for I had no one to counsel or comfort me. All I could do was pray God would protect me. The thought of losing the child early on occurred to me. I had heard of this happening often enough, but quickly dismissed it. I could never pray for such a thing, even though an unintended miscarriage would be a solution for which I would be grateful.

EARLY NOVEMBER - KINSALE

Within a few more days I accepted all hope was lost and decided my only choice was marriage. It seemed I must immediately accept Roland Fitzpatrick's offer and trust the three additional weeks required to announce the banns in church would not make the pregnancy seem too short. Roland would have to be convinced the child was conceived immediately after our marriage. It would mean the wedding must take place right after the third notification by the priest. I would be more than a month into the pregnancy. This would be cutting it close, but not unheard of, especially if I was fortunate enough to carry the child to full term and not have it come any earlier.

A glimmer of hope brightened my mood but for a moment. I also had to accept I was not looking forward to becoming his wife. Our world was in upheaval and I didn't want to leave my home and family yet. I just couldn't picture him offering me comfort, but he would offer me security and involuntarily legitimize the child I bore. I also dreaded fulfilling my duties as his wife. Now I knew the horror, pain and degradation entailed in the act, I had no desire to repeat it.

However, it was a sacrifice I needed to make to protect my dignity, my reputation and that of my family. I would tell my father of my decision to accept Roland's offer tomorrow after Mother and I returned from helping the Woman's Aid sewing group at church.

Meeting with the other women the next morning was a good distraction for me. We took bits and pieces of rags and worn out clothes and made new clothes, especially for children. This was even more important this year since all of us were eating much less than usual and the poor, ate barely anything at all. By keeping the young ones warmer, they were less likely to suffer. As the women chattered, I looked out the doorway and could see much activity as the troops scurried about repairing the cannon blasted walls.

Every day the English cannons would pound away at us. The Spanish troops would make forays into their front lines at night, kill as many as they could in the English trenches, sneak back and at dawn, repair the walls. I couldn't see how this was winning the war, but it was keeping the enemy at bay!

It was interesting, with the streets crowded, to see the stark difference between most of the fair-skinned, light haired locals and dark-haired Italians, Portuguese and Spanish. The variations of languages made an almost musical background noise. I stopped my sewing in mid-stitch. The importance of the difference instantly dawned on me in a brilliant flash of insight. The child I was carrying would almost certainly have de Avila's darker coloring. One often heard jests about a babe whose coloring didn't match the father. An image of Roland came to mind, fair of skin and hair, light blue eyes and tall. I quickly thought of my side of the family and couldn't think of one whose coloring went any darker than a light brown, or red gold. Roland was not the answer! My logical choice, my only choice, if I could, would be to select my dark-haired Thomas. I knew my father would be disappointed, not because he didn't like Thomas, but because Roland would be more secure and well placed in society.

"Oh! Thank God, I didn't go to Da yet about Roland. What a mistake it would have been." I realized.

Trying to find the right solution to my dilemma was becoming so complex. One lie after another. One plot after another and I knew there was more ahead of me!

Suddenly getting up, I said, "Ladies. Please excuse me, I think I need a bit of air."

I had to get away to think this through and the church room was suddenly too closed in and stuffy. I walked a short distance and sat on the steps in Market Square, anonymous and

immersed in the murmur of the crowd.

Keeping my fears and panic under control, I concentrated on how I would accomplish my goal. I knew some things were not in my power, but I would face those only if need be. First, I had to convince my father I had decided to accept Thomas's proposal. Father would be taken aback and would undoubtedly let me know he thought Roland's offer was, by far, the best choice. How could I persuade him otherwise? I would have to think more about it. This also assumed Thomas was still interested in marrying me. I didn't think his feelings had changed as he often showed me much affection and esteem. If this was so, I would then need to let Thomas know my preference and urge him to, once again, ask my father for my hand.

I could feel my anxiety lift a bit now I had dodged what could have been a serious mistake. I had little doubt Roland would have used me sorely, or perhaps even sent me back to my family in disgrace if he suspected the child was not his. I was starting to see possibilities with my new plan. Timing, yes, there was still the timing problem. I had to wed as soon as feasibly possible. The troublesome problem of a child born well before its time still loomed. I couldn't get back the days which had passed, but knew I had best approach Father this afternoon, without delay.

I said a silent prayer in hope God would give me the words I would need to make my case. If not, then God would have the more challenging task of helping me find the words to tell my parents I was ruined because of a vile rapist.

"You're rather quiet this morning. Is there something on your mind?" Mother asked as we walked toward home.

She had no idea! My mind was racing like a runaway horse. However, I thought this was a good opportunity to start laying some groundwork.

"I was wondering, Mother, what you think of Thomas Lydon?"

She stopped after a step or two and looked at me curiously.

"I'm quite fond of him, of course. He's been almost like part of this family since he was a lad and you and he played often when his family came calling." Smiling a bit, she said, "I remember his mother and I being concerned he was such a darlin' boy, that the lasses would be chasing after him and distract him from his studies."

I had to agree with her. I saw many of the young girls batting their eyelashes and finding excuses to talk to or taunt him. He was oblivious to all this female attention and they eventually gave up.

Mother went on to say, "He has been a loyal and hard-working assistant to your father for years too. His quick wits and education are far superior to older men, allegedly wiser. It's a shame his parents died when he was barely into manhood. They would have been so proud of him. Why the question, Fiona?"

"I have realized over several months my feelings for him are more than just friendship. This has been especially true since he has come to stay with us. I see how kind and polite he is and how Da counts on him. I've also noticed how warm and humorous he is when relaxed, even in these tense times. I was hoping to speak to Father about my relationship with Thomas, but I'm sure he'd prefer I marry Roland for many practical reasons."

I found weaving this tale to my mother upset me. We had, for the most part, a love based on trust and it saddened me to be manipulating her to help me hide my secrets. The only part which made it less painful was the fact that my feelings for Thomas had been growing to a more adult level. It was just this need to accelerate and coerce all involved which bothered me the most.

Thoughtfully, Mother explained, "There's no denying your Da is a practical man. He prefers to study all sides of an issue before making his decision. However, one thing to keep in mind is he loves you dearly and ensuring your happiness may well take precedence over some points. Let me reassure you, should your father ask my opinion, which is likely, I'll press for Thomas. Between you and me, I think Roland is a good businessman, but a pompous ass! When he is polite, I find him to be insincerely fawning and he strikes me as being quite more concerned with his needs and comforts first. Should something happen, and you do eventually wed Roland, you and I will immediately forget I spoke these opinions!"

My respect for my mother jumped to a new level. As her child, she usually felt obligated to always point out the best in others and use most opportunities to instill good Christian values in me. Today she treated me as an adult.

I found Thomas working over some books at the corner table to take advantage of the weak daylight. Laying my hand lightly on his arm I asked if he had a moment to speak with me privately. He looked up, surprised, but smiled and said what he was doing could wait. We stepped out into the walled part of the garden where the warmth of the sun didn't have to compete with the chilly breezes.

As we slowly walked the stone path, Thomas took my hand. With a concerned look on his face he asked "What's on your mind Fiona? Is it something which needs my help?"

"Well, it's certainly the truth of it! I need to speak to my father today. However, since the subject involves you, I need to discover your feelings first. My father told me of your tentative offer for my hand many months ago and I know he did not encourage you due to Roland's offer. What I want to tell you is I would like to accept your offer of marriage. Of course, if you are still interested in me as a wife."

Thomas stopped in mid-stride and looked at me in disbelief.

"Interested! How could I not be interested? I have loved you since we were too young to even know what love was. Are you serious? I mean truly serious?"

I now took both of his hands in mine. "Yes Thomas, I am."

"Fiona, my heart was broken when your father told me of Roland's offer, but I knew he could give you ever so much more than I and it would be a better match for the family. How could you settle for me and walk away from those advantages? That's not to say my heart isn't flying with hope right now. You know I would do anything to provide for and protect you. You are so dear to me and I cannot imagine being truly happy without you in my life."

I felt tears spring to my eyes at his words for I then knew I felt much the same way about him. I was so used to his being there for me, I never thought what it would be like if he was not. I leaned into his chest and he wrapped his arms around me. Kissing the top of my head, he said,

"Fi, you understand your father may not agree? He is struggling now with having to manage his business from afar for the Lynch's in Galway are handling his ships and cargo. In fact, it's one of the reasons we're so busy and are constantly communicating with him, Lynch is getting paid well for the use of his large warehouse and the additional workmen, but it's less costly than the sums we would lose trying to bring ships in and out of Kinsale. I'm afraid your father might think he would be insulting Roland by honoring your request to wed me and possibly ruining a business relationship once the troubles are over."

Drying my eyes, I looked up at him and said he might be right, but I must know. I planned on going to Da now and Thomas would hear from me soon, one way or the other.

"I think now I know what to say and I will do my best to get him to agree!" Kissing him quickly on the cheek, I dashed back into the house.

Father was home and I had to wait only a brief time to approach him after he had his mid-day meal and a glass of wine. This would be when he was most receptive. I entered the room with a warm smile on my face; looking up he returned it and motioned for me to come forward.

"Good afternoon Da. Is all well?"

"What with the bombardments and illness all about, I'm sure it could be better, but for me and mine, I think we're doing well. How about you me lovely daughter?"

I quickly sat on the footstool and placed my hand on his knee. "Father, I have come to a decision and it is my heart's desire you will be receptive to it."

His bushy brows raised a bit as he sensed my seriousness.

"Well, tell me child. You know I have nothing but your best interests in mind."

Taking a deep breath, with my heart pounding, I said "I have decided I wish to take Thomas Lydon as my husband.

Leaning forward with a quizzical look, he blurted out, "What? I don't understand!"

I explained, "I have spoken briefly with him and he seemed more than pleased at the prospect. However, I felt it would be best to speak with you before we made such a momentous decision."

"I should think so!" he said "What brought this on? You know I feel Thomas will do well in life and I know he's a good lad, but he can't give you the home, nor the status Roland can. Roland has even sworn to help defend Kinsale and personally promised to protect you. I feel he already sees you as his fiancée and envisions a merging of family and business." This could get nasty should I agree with your wish."

"I know Father, I know. However, I love Thomas and he is most kind and loving to me. I cannot say the same for Roland. I have always sensed he sees me more as a means to advance his business than as a loving partner. Your success in business is already secured without any merging with Roland. You may still wish to do so, but my being his wife is more to his advantage than to yours. Also, all our futures right now are known only to God and I wish to secure my place, not only with my family, but also with someone loving with whom I can share my life."

I could see Father's face soften as he listened to my plea.

"Oh Fiona," he said, placing his hand upon mine. "I don't know if you realize what you would be giving up. However, I know what it is to love, and I have been blessed to have married the woman who stole my heart so many years ago. I suggest you give it some further thought, then, if you still feel the same way in a month, or so, hopefully we'll be in a better place to plan a wedding and invite family."

No, no! This wouldn't do. I quickly prayed for God to give me the words I needed to turn this around. I spoke with nothing to go on but faith.

Trying to keep the panic out of my voice, I exclaimed "Father, I have already been thinking on this for quite a while and I wish to be wed as soon as possible. Our situation here grows more precarious by the day. There is hope the Irish forces will arrive, but that's all it is, hope! Food is diminishing, men are dying during skirmishes and disease is becoming rampant as the weather turns worse. Should something happen I do not want to be separated from Thomas. He already lives in our home and we can live here as easily as husband and wife as we are now. A large wedding means nothing to me as long as my immediate family is there to bless our union. Please let us take our joy in each other while we can so we may dream and plan of our future together."

With tears in his eyes, Father simply drew me to him and nodded yes. "Your mother will be none too pleased by missing out on wedding plans, however she's a practical woman and will see the wisdom of it. She'll get to spend my money on weddings soon enough, I'm sure, upon Chloe and Katy. If this is truly your wish, tell Thomas to come to see me in an hour. This will give me time to speak with your mother."

I was lightheaded with relief for I already knew Mother wouldn't try to dissuade him. I hugged him dearly and with much gratitude he loved me enough to unknowingly grant me the one thing which would save me.

I ran first to the walled garden and saw Thomas, despite the afternoon's damp chill, was still there. He was sitting on the stone bench, hunched over with his eyes closed and his elbows resting on his knees and his hands clasped at his chin. He felt my hand as I touched him on the shoulder and looked up into my face. His emotions were etched so strongly I was taken aback. Was it fear my father had agreed, or fear he had not?

"Father wants to see you in an hour. Unless mother changes his mind while we wait, Father has agreed to our marriage."

Such a glow of joy overtook his countenance I had no doubt where his heart lay.

"However," I interjected before he could utter a word, "I told him we should marry as soon as possible due to the upheaval and we would live here until we're able to make other plans, which may not be for quite a while. Would those arrangements be acceptable to you?"

Jumping to his feet, he picked me up and swung me around. Then he soundly kissed me. I was taken aback as much by the impulsiveness of his action as by the sweetness of the kiss.

"Oh Fiona! This is more than I could have hoped. I feel on top of the world and you'll be there with me. I can't see him for an hour? It will be the longest hour of my life."

However, it was not. For we spent the time holding hands and spoke of our suddenly different future together. We both agreed what we wanted most in this world was a home filled with love, happy children and a lack of want. Neither one of us could see where the current mayhem would lead us, but we shared a strong faith and decided it would be better to face it together.

However, I trusted Thomas would not sense my unease. I was troubled with guilt. My feelings for him were sincere, if not quite as deep as his seemed to be. However, I was entering this union dishonestly. I consoled myself with the knowledge that I had no other options besides total chaos and disgrace. I tried to tell myself I was really doing no actual harm unless my deception was discovered. I had already vowed to myself to go to the grave with my secret rather than hurt him and swore I would be as loyal and loving a wife as possible.

That afternoon Father and Mother blessed our plans and we moved on to making preparations. It was decided after the wedding, Chloe and Katy would move into the smaller room where Thomas now stayed, and he and I would have the larger room. Father apologized because he couldn't give his future son-in-law an increase in wages at this time, but of course we wouldn't expect him to since we would not have the expense of our own household. Mother took charge of the wedding plans and agreed to have Father request the first of the three required announcements be made by Father Milliken this Sunday. We could then wed any time after the third Sunday. Due to the war and dangers, we could only expect family and friends who already lived here be in attendance. I assured her I was more than satisfied with a smaller wedding. Thinking to myself this was another blessing as there was no need to allow more time before the wedding for people to arrive. As it was, I would be about five to six weeks along before we were wed. I knew there was no way around, but I had to admit it worried me All I could do was put it out of my mind for the moment and appreciated the fact of my plans playing out. The days now held promise and their passing took on a patina of normalcy and each one brought me closer to our wedding.

Don Aguila visited as often as he could for a congenial glass of wine in the comfort of a real home and to share his concerns. He fumed about losing more men to the cold, desertion and disease than to the skills of the English army. Dysentery was their enemy now, carrying off the ill-fed and weakened soldiers. They could tell by the burial details behind the lines that the English were also dealing with this dreaded illness. However, their losses didn't seem to be as extreme. By now, the promise of additional help from Spain was as likely to appear as a chorus of angels and the Irish were closer, but not yet on the scene.

After Don Aguila departed, Da shared this and other gossip with us at supper in the evening but I was very surprised when he said, "I must admit, I had to hide my temper when Aguila told me

several of our 'leading' citizens, packed up their possessions, including much needed livestock, and snuck away to Corke. Included in this esteemed group of cowards was our own, Roland Fitzpatrick; Protector of Kinsale and savior of the people! I couldn't even blame his departure on a broken heart as the scoundrel didn't know of your engagement Fiona. It won't be announced until this Sunday. It seems you made a wise choice in selecting Thomas, my dear."

Even though I wasn't completely shocked at Roland's departure, I had to admit I was disappointed he thought so little of his promises to me. I caught a quick look from Thomas which led me to believe he was checking to see how this news affected me. I trusted my smile of reassurance to him was enough.

MID-NOVEMBER - KINSALE

Our engagement was announced Sunday and Thomas and I were congratulated roundly. He was well-liked and everyone was more than ready for some good, happy news to offset the worsening conflict, weather and illness. Several of the men whisked Thomas off to stand him to a few drinks at the public house and I continued home with my parents. I truly felt God was blessing me with an unexpected future which would wash the stain from me, and I prayed I would be worthy of it.

As relieved as I was, I was still wrestling with the shorter time between our marriage and the estimated time of the babe's birth. In addition, I was also finding it more difficult to make myself get up in the morning these days. I was tired and groggy and then by early afternoon I was so fatigued I just wanted to lay where I was and go to sleep.

A few days after the Sunday announcement, I went to the kitchen for some ale, for it was the only thing which sounded good to me. Molly and Meg had already gotten a start on pickling some cabbage which had to be preserved before it rotted. I hadn't taken more than a few steps across the kitchen before the smell of the pungent cabbage and vinegar hit my nose and my stomach rebelled. This bit of warning sent me out to the privy on a run and I just made it before I vomited. At least no one saw me do so. I stayed until the cold sweats subsided and I felt my innards would stay where they belonged. I had heard about some women suffering from this odd ailment when expecting.

"Oh Lord," I thought "I hope this doesn't last through the whole time!"

Pinching my cheeks to give myself some color, I returned to the house, got a cup of beer and a crust of bread, and took it upstairs. I nibbled a bit on the crust and was able to keep it down. I needed to know more about this new concern.

Later in the day, when I was feeling more myself, I wandered out to the back where Meg was laying clothes out to dry on the shrubbery. Offering to help, I struck up a conversation with her. This was easy enough as she loved to have someone besides Molly with whom to share the latest tales. We discussed this and that for a while when I finally shared, "By the way Meg, when I was out the other day, I saw a poor lass become ill in the street. I felt so sorry for her to be seen in such a condition. Do you suppose she was sick from one of the terrible illnesses going around?"

Meg's ear perked up. She loved hearing something colorful and to be asked for her opinion was even better.

"Well, true it is that the bloody flux is taking men down like a scythe, but I hear it knocks those getting it down so fast they wouldn't be likely to be wandering around the streets. Did this lass look quite sickly and weak?

I paused a moment to appear as though I was recalling an actual scene before I answered.

"No. I don't think so. It seemed to have struck her suddenly and with no time to find a more private place to retch. Of course, she was quite pale, but I suppose such would be understandable."

"Ah well," Meg said with a voice of authority. "I would think it is more likely she might simply be expecting a child and was suffering a new mother's illness."

Just the lead-in I needed!

"Oh my. Is it quite common? It would seem women wouldn't be able to get anything done if they spent the whole time ill in their stomach."

I made sure I sounded completely ignorant of the ways of pregnancy, which wasn't far from the truth.

"No, no," Meg went on to explain. "Some women never have a moment of it, others for just a few weeks and some for several months. Although, I have known some who stayed quite ill the whole time. They usually had wee and frail babes due to not being able to hold their food down."

"Oh dear! Isn't there something a poor lass can do to avoid this?"

The thought of trying hide my new ailment was daunting enough, but to think it might last for months was something I didn't want to contemplate.

"Me sister Colleen and some others I know of say chewing fennel seeds, or beer made from mint helped. I remember she used to keep a bit of dried bread next to her bed. She would eat some of the bread even before she arose. Unfortunately, the availability of dried bread also brought in mice!"

I recalled the piece of bread I had eaten did seem to help. I had a tin I could keep in my drawer upstairs which would give me place for bread and avoid the mouse problem Meg's sister had. We had a good supply of dried herbs from our garden so I would try Meg's remedies right away.

As Thomas and I spent more time together, our affection grew, and we started sharing a kiss or two when we could. I noticed he was finding more and more opportunities to hold my hand, brush a strand of my hair off my face, or simply sit closer to me on the bench. The family was also treating him more like a son, than a friend, or employee and Chloe and Katy loved teasing me by calling him brother Thomas already. However, as each weekday slipped away, the more concerned I became about my biggest problem. It was obvious I needed to make a bold move.

As much as I dreaded it, I realized the answer lay in coming up with some way to make Thomas be intimate with me for he was the one who needed to be sure the child was his. Although I used to be shocked by it, I wasn't so ignorant to think all couples waited until their vows were said. I wasn't sure if tricking him was possible since he had always been a man known for his good character. I couldn't envision him taking advantage of me, but de Avila's animal brutality certainly proved I didn't understand the ways of men. I suspected, should my plan work, no matter how repulsive the experience might be, it couldn't be as horrid as the Spaniard's attack.

At least I would have an idea of what was going to happen and be more prepared. I also consoled myself knowing Thomas was, without a doubt, a gentler soul.

I spent all day in a quandary feeling guilt for brazenly planning on committing this sin. The assault was not my fault and I had tried to accept God's forgiveness. However, this plot would be done with forethought and I would be tempting Thomas to commit a sin. On the other hand, it was far worse to risk the pain Thomas would feel if he discovered this was not his child and to realize I willingly led him into marriage under false circumstances. The two, or so extra weeks this would buy me would be worth it. After much anguish, I accepted I would rather disappoint God, than Thomas. I felt God would be more likely to forgive me.

Two nights later appeared to be a good opportunity. There was a storm blowing and the winds caused the house to creak and moan which would make my walk to his room less likely to be noted. The coldness should also encourage the household to stay bundled up in their beds and less likely to investigate any strange movement.

I lay in bed, tense and apprehensive, waiting for all to settle down for the night. Chloe and Katy were already snuggled together, snoring softly. I tiptoed to the door, opened it gently and noticed there was still a flicker of candlelight showing beneath Thomas's door. I would have to check again later. I didn't want to catch him at his work, nor did I have the courage to walk into his room in the light.

I wrapped myself in my coverlet and stood waiting and watching. It was only a short while before the light went out. I waited a little longer for him to get settled. Removing my coverlet, I walked silently toward his door.

I could feel the rough boards beneath my feet and the frigid air in the hallway seeped quickly through my thin linen shift. By now I was trembling, but it wasn't only from the cold. I nearly turned back in fear and would have if my situation had not been so dire. I entered his room and stood just inside the door. I could tell he was in bed and saw him slowly raise his head to see who had entered.

"What ho? Who's there? "

The fire on the grate had burned down but provided enough light to see. His eyes widened as he recognized me. Sitting up, he asked me, "Fiona? Is that you? Why are you here? What's wrong? "

I took a few steps toward him and softly said, "There's nothing wrong; at least, there's no danger. I must speak with you though in private. I hope you'll forgive me for coming to you this late."

"No, no. it's no problem. What is troubling you so?"

I came closer and was now standing next to his bed.

"Thomas, this is a delicate subject, but since we are to be man and wife, I trust you will not think me too forward to broach it. The fact of the matter is I am frightened."

"Frightened!" he exclaimed, taking my hand "Of what? Do you feel it would be a mistake to marry me? Have you changed your mind?"

"No Thomas, not at all."

There was relief in his voice "Well, I'm glad of that to be sure. Oh Fiona, you're shivering ever so much."

He pulled me down to sit on the bed and put a corner of his bedcover over my shoulders.

"Now I know you won't be throwing me aside, I will try to calm whatever bothers you,"

Taking a deep breath, I told him, "I want to be a good wife to you, but I am afraid of what goes on between a man and wife in the bedroom. I have heard disturbing tales of pain, and women finding it to be a burdensome obligation. I don't want it to be so to me, but I don't understand what is expected. I cannot ask my Mother for it is too private a thing."

"Oh, my dearest Fiona. It's no wonder you are frightened. I won't deny your fears are not entirely unfounded in some marriages, but it doesn't have to be so. Caring deeply for each other, as we do, helps and we have also had the advantage of spending much time together, so have learned to be more comfortable together. The act of love, and this is what it should be, is more a physical thing and I think there is some discomfort for the woman the first time. If the husband is gentle and takes his time, it should be less so. It should then become more and more pleasurable for both."

Thomas had left his arm about my shoulders when he placed the bed cover on me. I could feel the warmth of him next to him and knew he could feel mine too.

"What if I don't know what to do? What if I don't please you?" I asked.

"Oh, dearest Fi, we will learn how to please each other. It's the beauty of it for it's not only the making love which creates the intimacy. It's knowing at the end of the day you have someone to share your thoughts; make your plans together and with whom to discuss your worries."

Laying my head on his shoulder, I thanked him softly for his reassurances. Then it was only a slight move on my part to place my lips on his. I heard a slight intake of breath before he returned the kiss with the sweetness I recalled in the garden. Emboldened, I place my hand on the nape of his neck, feeling the soft feathering of his hair on my fingers and let my lips press more firmly and with more fervor. He responded by sliding his hand from my shoulder to my back, drawing me closer to him. I could feel my breasts now pressed against him and he was the one starting to tremble.

"Fiona, do you have any idea how beautiful you are?" he whispered in my ear. "I thought you were an angel standing at my door. The dying coals were sending glints of fiery golden lights playing in your hair. Ah; your hair. I haven't seen it flowing so long and softly about your shoulders since you were a wee lass." Nuzzling his nose into my curls, he asserted it was softer than the finest silk and smelled of the most heavenly herbs.

Thomas's breathing became more rapid as he laid his hand on my thigh. A soft moan emanated from his throat. He suddenly pulled back and admitted he was taking things too far, although his eyes were lit with an eagerness which was inviting and kind. Not the cold, hard gaze I saw in de Avila's face. I quickly closed my eyes and forced the ugly picture back into the dark corner of my mind where it belonged.

When I opened my eyes again, all I saw was love and desire in Thomas. His hand moving slowly and sensuously on my thigh belied his weak declaration to resist. Without thought, I knew what I would say next was what his heart wanted to hear.

"Thomas. Show me how you will be gentle with me. Let me know I'm safe with you."

I could feel his excitement rise, his desire to please me overtaking his reluctance. I was also experiencing new feelings. His kisses moved from my mouth trailing down to my throat. He reached up and untied the neck of my gown. I tensed as he reached for my breast, anticipating the pain I had experienced with de Avila's cruel grasp. But his was different. His caress was gentle and even though my breasts were becoming tender due to my condition, this seemed to only increase the pleasure. Kissing me again on the mouth, he gradually pressed me back onto the mattress, continuing his intriguing exploration. A dreamy state was overtaking me, and a languid warmth ran through my body, totally unfamiliar to me, but quite pleasant.

He did take his time, however I didn't have to pretend discomfort as he entered me, for this physical intrusion was still new to me. The blessing was, after the caresses, the embraces seemed natural and comfortable. Within moments I sensed a buildup of tension and purpose from him and then the release. With a deep sigh, he lowered himself to lay next to me.

I was overcome by the realization that, not only was my mission accomplished, but I now knew I had nothing to fear from him. Suddenly, tears sprang to my eyes with the relief I felt. Thomas reached for me and said, "Oh my sweet girl. I'm so sorry. I shouldn't have done such a thing. I should have stopped myself, but I have wanted you for so long and to have you in my arms was such a gift. How can you forgive me?"

"Thomas, Thomas, don't feel so! This was my fault as much as, if not more so, than yours. I now understand it was wrong to tempt you by coming to your room. But I'm not sorry I did for you have shown me I've nothing to fear and this will make our wedding day all the sweeter."

"But Fiona, according to the church, we've sinned! Although, it doesn't feel like a sin to me."

Smiling, I lay my head on his chest and told him I doubted we would be the first couple to confess such a transgression to Father Milliken and he and God would forgive us."

Hugging me to him, he murmured "Yes. I believe you're right. But, as much as I hate to say this, we mustn't do this again until we are wed. Perhaps you can wear your most unbecoming clothes and keep your hair under a kerchief and smudge your face, so you won't be so unbelievably lovely to me!"

Smiling, he kissed the top of my brow and then softly on my eyelids.

"Go," he begged, "before I lose my head as I've lost my heart! I will dream sweet dreams of you tonight, my love."

I was reluctant to leave his arms and the warm nest in which we snuggled. However, I knew he was right, plus the longer I stayed, the more chance there was someone would notice my absence.

What a difference there was in my return to my room. I felt as though the weight of the world had been lifted from my shoulders. The child might now be considered an early delivery and Thomas could truly believe we conceived it this very night. I slept deeply in peace for the first time since the attack. I arose the next morning with prayers for forgiveness and full of praise for my rescue. Thomas and I shared secret glances and smiles throughout the following days but were very careful to avoid any opportunities to be alone.

Our wedding day on November 28th dawned bright and clear with a light dusting of snow which gave everything a fresh clean look. The scars of battle were somewhat hidden, and all looked hopeful again. Mother, Chloe and Katy fussed over me as I dressed. Mother had added a pale blue strip of wool along the front panels of my sea-green cloak and used matching material on the kirtle of my gown. Colum and Robbie had gone through their chests and put together a very handsome suit of clothing for Thomas. Molly, who was very handy with a needle, made some adjustments in the fit and it truly flattered Thomas's slim build. The doublet of fawn accented his eyes and the deep blue trim went well with his lovely hair. Da loaned him his finest full cape trimmed with fur. My father proudly wore his velvet hat. It had a medium crown and small brim. But the bragging point was the expensive peacock feather stuck in the hat. As bright as skies were now, no one living in Ireland would be ever assume the weather wouldn't change. The clouds out to sea were a roiling gray and the wind was blowing them inland. I suspect in a sudden deluge, Da would be inclined to save his special hat before thinking to save anyone else! Mam would not be outdone either. She had added some lovely stitching to the sleeves of her turquoise dress and had even stuffed them to fill them out in the Elizabethan fashion. She had covered her hair with a French hood. The oval crown framed her face beautifully and the long veil down the back sheathed the length of her hair and kept it in place.

Though I wasn't supposed to eat before the wedding Mass, I had nibbled on my hidden stash of bread in hopes of keeping my nausea at bay. It seemed to be working with only a few, to be expected, butterflies to contend with.

Immediate friends and family gathered at our home to walk with us to the church. I was most grateful for the crisp cold air for I was feeling quite strange. It was as though I was just floating through the actions without really being part of them. I could barely grasp the knowledge I would be a married woman in just a few hours. My childhood would be behind me, motherhood loomed in the very near future and I would be bound to another for the rest of my life.

Quite a few of our other friends and neighbors joined us in the procession and I could tell Mother was pleased. However, we were both surprised the church already held a large number of Kinsale's citizens when we arrived. They and those with us all found places to stand. The winter sunlight backlit the stained-glass windows and it was easy to believe we were in one of the finest of cathedrals. Father had included some music to open the ceremony, I remained at the back of the church until all was settled and the entrance hymn was sung. Father was with me and I was straining to see if I could locate Thomas, but the crowd was too thick. The hymn ended and a hush came over the crowd. My heart was beating as fast as a sparrow's. Feeling a bit lightheaded, I tightly grasped my father's arm. He leaned down, kissed the top of my head and said,

"Look for Thomas and keep your eyes on him, Fiona. Think of nothing else."

The crowd parted then and Father and I slowly marched forward. Ah! There he was, standing straight and so handsome next to Father Milliken. Just then he looked up and saw me. His face was a bit pale, but his smile lit up the room. My feet steadied, and my heart slowed to a more normal beat. Even though our path starting here might be full of pits and dangerous turns, I knew in this moment here was a man I could trust, learn to love and one who would protect me and what was to become our child. God had answered my prayers and now I must fulfill my promises to be the best wife and mother I could be. Da leaned down, with tears in his eyes, and said he loved me and would pray for me, then handed me to Thomas.

During the vows, my voice was shaky but clear. Thomas's rang with a confidence which made me smile. Most of the wedding passed in a blur. I could hear Mother muffling her tears and little Katy's voice would pipe up in a loud whisper periodically asking Chloe about the ceremony. I didn't dare glance at my dear loved ones as I was afraid it would be the undoing of what little composure I had. I kept reminding myself how fortunate I was to not have to leave my family and the comfort of my home directly after being wed.

Molly, Meg and Bridie only stayed long enough to see the exchanging of the vows and ring, and then hurried home to finish the preparations for the wedding supper. As limited as food was, I knew my mother would dig into her hidden stores and Bridie would work her magic to make the mundane look like a royal feast.

The winds picked up, the clouds got heavier and closer, but held off. Thomas and I led the march back uphill followed by a quite accomplished group of local lads playing some gay and wonderful airs and ballads. I glanced behind us and almost laughed at the number of people trudging with us. It appeared everyone but the halt and the lame in Kinsale would bless our marriage today. Thomas held my hand firmly and asked how I was doing.

"As hard as it is to believe, considering how nervous I was just a few hours ago, right now all I am is hungry! I trust there won't be many toasts before some food is served or I may swoon, and you'll have to carry me upstairs to lay with a cold cloth on my head."

With a chuckle and a grin, he whispered,

"Milady, I have every intention of carrying you upstairs and we can dispense with the cold cloth! I will, however, allow you to eat first as I believe you will want to keep up your strength."

Fortunately, there was no one in front of us to witness my blush.

The party was grand, and Father had gotten several bottles of his finest wine for the initial toasts. After, it was beer, ale and local whiskies which fueled the festivities, someone even donated a cask of mead, which we all agreed as most appropriate since it is considered the 'honeymoon' drink. The foods were a special treat to most, and more than one morsel found its way into a pocket or pouch for later.

As the time wore on there was an increase in ribald stories and innuendo, many of which I couldn't quite guess the meaning. My father sensed when it might go too far and advised Thomas and I me to scurry quietly away upstairs. He said our room (the one I used to share with my sisters) had been prepared. He shook Thomas's hand and with damp eyes, gave me another hug and a blessing.

Apparently, the women of the household had been busy upstairs too. We smiled when we entered what was now our home within the house. The two small beds had been replaced with one larger bed. Everything was dusted and polished. There were no flowers this time of year, but someone had tied sturdy, fragrant, rosemary branches into bundles wrapped with colorful ribbons and placed them around the room plus one each on our pillows. A new privacy screen painted with brilliant birds was set up in the corner. The peat fire was lit, and the room was as cozy as could be. Thomas set down the candle he had carried up and blew it out.

"I don't think we'll need this, he said softly. The fire will allow us enough light to prevent us having to play 'Blind Man's Bluff'. He wrapped his arms around me and asked if I realized I was the most beautiful bride ever?

"All I knew," I answered, "was a very handsome man was waiting for me at the end of the aisle and I had better wed him before the other lasses realized their loss!"

He kissed me long and slowly and I was more than willing to return the favor. Pulling his face back from mine he said "I know this has been a very long and busy day. However, I am hoping you are not too tired to make a leisurely night of it for I have dreamt of discovering you as a woman and as my wife. Don't get me wrong," he smiled, "I have no complaints about our first time together, but this will be so much more."

He lifted my cloak from my shoulders and laid it on a chair and looked admiringly at the low-cut neckline of my gown. He made a bit of a humming noise as he ran his fingers down from my throat and across the tops of my breasts where they mounded above the dress. I found this to be most pleasant and relaxing. However, I was also experiencing an unusual feeling of liquid warmth embracing me. The more he kissed and caressed me, the more my body responded and encouraged me to hold and caress him.

He suddenly stepped away from me and I experienced a brief sense of loss as our embrace was broken. Thomas let out a sigh and whispered,

"I need to slow down a moment Fiona. I am almost overcome with the sweet smell and feel of you in my arms."

He reached into his doublet and pulled out a small flask. He poured two wee drams and handed me one.

"Here. Take a sip of this while I get out of this doublet and ruff. I must admit they are quite uncomfortable and will definitely get in the way of my planned explorations."

I realized he was right. My mind and body were both in a pleasant and powerful turmoil. I took a sip and felt the delightful fire of an excellent brandy as it coursed down my throat and settled like a warm pool in my belly. Thomas wasted no time in disrobing and before I knew it, he was standing in front of me wearing nothing but his linen shirt, which hung to about mid-calf. He quickly downed his drink and reached for the laces on my bodice. He slowly untied them, his fingers dancing softly against my skin. I closed my eyes immersing myself in his tantalizing touch. I felt him slowly pushing the material away and exposing my breasts. He let out a deep breath and I looked at him. He was not looking at my face now.

"Ah! So beautiful. So perfect." He sighed, cupping them gently.

He lowered his head and slowly kissed each nipple, stroking each one with his tongue. I was now trembling with emotion and feared my legs would no longer support me. Thomas must have sensed this for he quickly removed my gown, picked me up in his arms and carried me to the bed. We were now in a frenzy of need and mutually caught up in the sensuality of enjoying each other with abandon. In exhaustion and release, we eventually fell to sleep in each other's arms. We awoke again in the wee hours of the night and enjoyed the dance of love to a slower rhythm.

The morning sun roused me, and it took a few moments for me to realize I wasn't waking from a dream, but I was now married. I glanced over at Thomas and he was still asleep. His lovely hair was tousled, and his face was fully relaxed in slumber. This gave me an opportunity to study him more closely. His lips were soft and full, more so than I had ever noticed before. The cover only came up to his middle and I noticed the hair on his chest was blue black, just like on his head, but was sparser, not a thick mat like my oldest brother's reddish tangles. I reached over and gently ran my hand over the hair and liked the softness. I smiled when I noticed how it made little swirls around his nipples.

It was well past the time I normally rose, so I thought I'd best get up. It abruptly occurred to me when I went downstairs, everyone would know what transpired between the two of us. A blush bloomed on my face.

"I hope I'm the cause of those rosy cheeks, Fiona."

Thomas had awakened, unbeknownst to me, and was looking at me with a cat-like grin.

"You are in a way, you rascal. It was just occurring to me the family will know what we have been doing up here and I'm embarrassed to go downstairs."

He let loose with a melodic laugh and declared he would go downstairs as proud as a rooster. "After all, it isn't every man who gets to bed a woman as lovely as you and you're mine forever!"

He reached for me and start nuzzling and cooing when I pushed him away.

"No, no Thomas, we mustn't. Everyone's up and they'll hear us. Plus, the longer I stay up here, the more embarrassing it will be to go downstairs!"

I also knew I needed to get a bit of beer and toast to settle my stomach. So far, I had been fortunate to only suffer a little from the upset stomach in the morning.

"You're a cruel, mean woman," he groaned "to leave a man in such a condition. Have you no heart, no sympathy, no compassion?"

I couldn't help but laugh but insisted I must face the family and do my household duties. He did manage to give me a sound smack on my backside as I slipped out of bed and I have to say, it made me feel quite the married woman.

All were busy in the kitchen when I got there so I quietly went about my business of fixing a bite to eat. Although I appreciated the lack of attention, their quietness was a little disconcerting. Then, on a secret signal, Mother, Meg and Molly all turned to me and said,

"Sure, and it's a good morning to you, Mistress. Lydon!"

There was another blush creeping up my face. I wondered how long it would take me to get used to my new name and position. Mother was smiling, but I recognized the penetrating look she had always used when trying to determine my innermost feelings without being bold enough to ask. The hint of a cloud passed within moments and a look of contentment and relief replaced any doubts she may have harboured. The ladies were kind enough to not make reference to the wedding night, but knowing grins flitted between them like happy butterflies.

All tension was relieved when Thomas came blustering into the kitchen and, in a loud voice, demanded, "Where's my breakfast beer and bread, woman! Your husband is nearly faint with hunger."

He went around and gave each of us a kiss as we laughed at his antics.

Life went on as before, and I waited for a while before letting Thomas know I suspected I was with child and it may have been conceived on our first night together, although there had been plenty of opportunities for conception since the wedding.

Shock registered upon his face. "What? So soon? Of course, I know there's no set time once a marriage is consummated. But, I, well, I guess I never thought so far ahead."

"Oh Thomas, I know this is not a convenient time, but, if I'm right, nature will take its course." In fact, just in case I'm wrong, it would be best to wait a bit longer for proof I am or am not expecting a child. I'm sorry this caught you unawares."

By now he was smiling. Pulling me closer to him, he said, "Don't be sorry darlin'. A child is always a blessing and your family will be over the moon to welcome their first grandchild into their home. Babies don't take up much room so he, or she, will simply stay in our room."

A crease appeared between his eyes as a thought occurred to him.

"I've heard there are ways to determine if the babe is to be a boy, or a girl. Do you think we can find out?"

I giggled a bit and told him those were mostly old wife's tales. After all, there was always a fifty per cent chance they would be right!

"Ah! No matter," he said, "It will be loved and will be a blessing as we start our family."

A tear glinted in his eyes and he said he wished his parents could have lived to see this.

He kissed me long and sweetly and whispered in my ear, "I know we should wait, but truth be told, I want to tell everyone I know! When will it be born?"

This is where I had to careful. I needed to be vague and remind him of the possibility the child was conceived two weeks before the wedding.

"We're going have to say about August for you know how people start counting to see when the first child is born. There is a chance this could have happened before we were wed. Fortunately, once the child comes, no one is overly concerned about anything but the health of the wee one."

His faced suddenly flushed a bit, recollecting our first encounter. Such thoughts apparently led him to his next question. and he asked, rather fearfully, if being intimate now would harm the babe. I reassured him, unless the mother was experiencing problems, we would be able to continue to enjoy each other through most of my confinement and his main problem might be that he won't want me when I got fat!

Relieved, he hugged me again and declared, "I like women with a little meat on their bones. Makes them more comfortable for snuggling."

An excellent answer, I thought!

It was just before mid-December when we shared the news with our family. My mother threw her apron to her face and started crying, which concerned me until I heard her saying,

"Jesus, Mary, and Joseph! Thank you for this blessing."

Father, on the other hand, hugged us both soundly and kept shaking Thomas's hand and congratulating him with such pride, you'd have thought he'd sailed to France in a tub! Mother started dithering about clothes, gowns. knitting and having father drag out Katy's cradle to be redone. Then her face lit up even more and She said, "Oh my! Won't I just be having something to share at the Women's Guild this week!"

Ever since Thomas and I decided to marry, all had fallen into place and life seemed to go forward as though there was nothing hidden in the past. Despite the depravations of war, I could now look forward to basking in my role as wife and mother to be. Unfortunately, this was not quite how it worked out.

MID-DECEMBER – A MESSAGE ARRIVES

As we ate yet another meal of fish, oatcakes and pickled vegetables, I tried to remember to be grateful we lived where there was a steady supply of fish. Mutton and beef were in scant supply. Those who had milk cows were protecting them like a hoard of gold, which made sense since the price for milk had escalated and to slaughter them now would mean no milk in the future. The other good news for those with cows was the number of cattle stolen and/or slaughtered, by both sides, provided more winter fodder for those who remained.

The same was happening with sheep. The breeding stock was also being protected to provide more lambs. To have a ewe give birth to a single lamb was good news, to have twins was grand, but on the rare occasion she gave birth to three at a time, the farmer was certainly expected to celebrate his good fortune with a pint for himself and his boyos.

This miserable winter was taking its toll on both the English and the Spanish forces. From October on there had been several major battles, with the Spaniards and their multinational forces, surprising the English with their cunning and bravery as well as dozens of nighttime raids diminishing Mountjoy's men in the trenches. These sallies were successful in keeping the troops further away from access to Kinsales ancient and precarious walls, but at the cost of losing many of Aguila's men too. The diseases which are caused by a lack of food, clean water, warm clothing, plus large groups of people crammed together in each other's waste, continued unabated and were now spreading amongst the citizens of Kinsale. The Irish Forces had finally arrived but had not engaged Mountjoy in a major battle yet. Aguila was feeling emboldened as O'Neill and the others started putting pressure on the English troops north of Kinsale, while the Spanish forces, with renewed vigor, increased the pressure from the south. It was during this time we heard from an unexpected source and our lives took a surprising turn.

About three in the afternoon, on December 10th, Father and Thomas burst in through the front door, out of breath and with steam rising from their snow-dampened clothes.

"Fiona!" called Thomas.

"Mary! Come quickly!" echoed my father. "We've just received some dispatches from Galway. Andrew Lynch says the Irish forces, now in the south, are playing mayhem with shipping and manpower. He says many of the young men in Galway and Limerick have left to join the Chieftains as they make their way to Kinsale. Three of them were clerks in his employ and he is hard put to keep track of his own ships and cargoes, let alone mine. He has asked we send Thomas to Galway, forthwith, to take charge of our accounts."

"Oh Thomas!" I gasped "How long will you be gone? Will you be safe there?"

He had me in his arms in two steps. "Sit down Fiona. These are just the questions I had, and I need to discuss some options with you. Of course, my first thought was to leave you in the care of your parents and try to get back as soon as possible. However, after much thought, I think we must do the following. We have no idea how long this battle, or for that matter, this war will last, and I have no desire to leave my wife, especially in your condition, for a long time. But, uppermost in my mind is the advanced deterioration of our safety here. You and the babe would be exposed to widespread illness and, God forbid, English forces taking over Kinsale. I have told your father I want us to leave for Galway together before your condition makes it impractical. I also recommended they do so the same. There is nothing we can do now to make a difference in the defense of the town, and we must do what we can to protect ourselves and your father's business from Galway."

"Oh! How horrid. But, but where will we live, what do we take? How long must we stay? Mother, you all must come too."

By now mother was leaning against father and crying. "Oh Francis, we can't possibly uproot our children and move a household to Galway within weeks, let alone days! but, I can't bear to have Fiona so far away and not knowin' if I will even see her before, or after, the babe is born." She sobbed even harder now.

Thomas reached over and touched mother's hand. "Milady, Andrew has offered us quarters with Christopher Lynch at their family castle, in Galway and Fiona will be well cared for there. Galway doesn't seem to be overly affected by these events beyond some shortages. I will promise you this. If you stay here, I will do everything possible to bring Fiona home for the birth. This will be many months away and we can hope whatever the outcome is, Kinsale will be out of the worst of it by then. However, I cannot promise, so you and Francis will need to talk. Fiona and I will retire to our room to give you privacy.

With much anguish and sorrow, it was decided Thomas and I would pack our personal possessions and leave within three days. Thomas and Da spent much of their time pouring over documents, invoices, manifests etc. It was also agreed my brother Colum would step in to help father. He had been helping Da around the ships for years and he had developed a fair hand at record keeping. They would also start training Robbie. Mother, Chloe, Katy and I spent half the time mending and packing and the other half crying. Poor wee Katy was clingy and cross at the turmoil. Even Colum and Robbie were solemn, and I caught some tears in their eyes also. Much too soon it was time to leave. We were wrapped in several layers of robes against the bitter early morning cold and Mother handed us a hamper filled with enough food to sustain us between stops.

Da gave Thomas a generous purse for shelter and food along the way and advised, "If the weather holds Thomas, you should arrive in about a week. The money I gave you should allow for staying at decent inns along the way and a hot supper."

The money and anything of value were now secreted in a compartment under a false floor in the wagon. Thomas was not without weapons, but we did our best to look rather bedraggled and without any goods to discourage any brigands who might be on the road. We finally had to pull ourselves away and did so after many hugs, promises to write and heartfelt thanks for all they had done.

We were very quiet for the first hour, or so, but it wasn't long before the steady pace on the road and changing scenery gave us the feeling of progress and our conversation picked up, turning from the difficulty of leaving our home to what type of work he'd be doing for Lord Lynch. I found this to be quite interesting as I really didn't know how such records helped a merchant. It wasn't something Da felt needed to be shared with his daughters. Thomas also told me wonderful stories of his time in Galway when he was there to study and the sights, he would show me. He had stayed with the Lynch's then too and reassured me they would do all they could to make me feel welcome. I must admit it sounded quite exciting. I was nervous, but also looking forward to seeing such a large city.

The weather stayed cold and we had to put up with a few showers before we finally got to a waystation where we could spend the night. I had never spent the night outside of Kinsale and was concerned about the safety of such an establishment. However, by the time we got there, the well-lit windows and a promise of a fire, food and a bed eased my fears quite a bit. Thomas was familiar with this process and reassured me a few coins would ensure our wagon and horse would be properly cared for and a decent room secured for us. He explained the meal would probably be hearty and good, but the accommodations would not be elegant, nor even overly clean, nevertheless there would be nothing to fret about.

I was a bit taken aback upon entering the Inn. It was quite busy and noisy. Thomas explained this inn served many who were not only going north, but also those going southeast toward Corke. From the sounds, most of the travelers were very pleased to be out of the weather. Thomas spotted a young woman who was obviously serving the guests. He led me over to her and asked if there was a decent, private room available and we would also want a meal. She didn't say anything, just bobbed a curtsey and left.

I looked at Thomas anxiously. "Why did she just go? It's very busy; what if there are no rooms?"

"Such usually isn't the case. Many are here just for the food and drink, and most of those staying can only afford a room shared with any number of strangers. Those with even less will be allowed to curl up in a corner on the floor. The serving girl went to find the proprietor for she would not be aware of what was or was not available."

Quite relieved, I spent the next few minutes noticing my surroundings. The furnishings of tables and benches were rude, but functional. The tables which seemed to seat the largest groups were also the ones where the patrons were mostly involved in drinking and dicing. No one appeared to be concerned about the tabletops being puddled with spilled wine and ale. However, many of the smaller tables, with only two to four people, were wiped clean more often and had a decent candle on each. A large stone fireplace was situated behind a long board which separated the common room from the barrels and cooking area. There were many chickens and various large pieces of meat on spits over the fire. I felt my mouth suddenly fill with saliva which registered how very, very, hungry I was. A red-faced man wearing a well-used apron and with sweat upon his brow came up to us, made a slight brow and announced. "Good even sir.

Bessy tells me you need a room and a meal? Will this just be for the two of you?"

"Aye," said Thomas "A private room if you please for my wife and me, some mulled ale and a hot meal at the small table in the corner. Also, I have stabled my wagon and one horse with your man outside. We will be leaving first thing in the morning."

The man's bestubbled face beamed broadly showing a fair number of gaps in his smile.

"Ah! Tis no problem, Bessy will set you at the table and bring your fare and I will prepare a room." He then threw his chest out and proudly announced. "I will place a clean sheet on yer bed!"

This appeared to be a great concession and was meant to earn a little extra on the bill, but Thomas took it in stride. They settled on a sum and the proprietor dramatically escorted us to our table. Bessy soon scooted over to us with two mugs of spiced ale and a hot poker. When she plunged the poker into the ale, the aroma was heavenly. A bowl of broth, bread and a plate of fowl and mutton were soon added, and Thomas and I attacked it as though we had starved for a week. After a bit, I took a few moments to look at the people scattered about the inn. There were few women and most of the people were dressed a little worse for wear than the clothing we had chosen. There were also a number who showed abject poverty. Even in this weather some had no shoes and wore only long shirts over trews. Some wore hosen, but they were more holes than cloth. I then noticed one of these looking overlong at us from under his floppy hat. Embarrassed, I looked away, but as is a human habit, I glanced back later and again caught him giving us a serious once over.

"Thomas?" I said leaning toward him. "There's a man with a large soiled leather hat to my right who seems quite interested in us."

Oddly, Thomas took my hand as though whispering sweet nothings to me and giving me a rather inane smile, he said, "Do not look at him. I have already noticed him and prefer he not be aware of us spotting him." Kissing the back of my hand, he went right back to his supper.

A bit more than halfway through this surprisingly tasty meal, the warm, smoky room, mug of ale and buzz of conversation made my eyelids seem very heavy.

Thomas gently pointed out sunrise would come sooner than we would like, and it would be best to retire before I fell asleep on the table. There was no argument from me. As we headed up the stairs, Thomas, turned toward the back board and rather loudly called out.

"Innkeeper, if you will, please don't awaken us early. My wife is exhausted, and we would prefer to leave for Corke about mid-morning." As I started to ask him if he'd gone daft, he firmly squeezed my arm and led me up the stairs. Upon entering our room, he explained he felt the man had shown much too much interest in us and noted we had the wherewithal to pay for a room and supper. Therefore, it would be best if the fellow thought he would have plenty of time to follow us without having to get up at the crack of dawn and he would, hopefully try to find us on the road to Corke, not Galway.

"He's undoubtedly ordered another drink by now imagining he would have a leisurely night's sleep and some stolen coins in his pocket by mid-day! We, on the other hand, will leave before light and be hours away before his head clears."

Our room was quite small and chilly, but there was a surprisingly substantial blanket on the bed and two small pillows which would at least provide us with the impression of comfort. The linens were quite gray, but as promised, fairly clean. I don't think my head had even reached the pillow before I slept. We quietly slipped away just before sunrise, as planned and noticed the wily fellow snoring away under a table as we left the inn.

We made good headway the next two days and were enjoying a lack of rain. As much as I was appreciating the changes in scenery as we headed north, I felt a bit melancholy. It finally occurred to me I could no longer smell the sea and it seemed most strange. Thomas reassured me the scent which had always been in my life would be present again in Galway.

"Thomas? Why would people abandon their homes?"

"What? We're not abandoning our home Fiona!"

"No Thomas. I don't mean us. It's just I've been seeing more and more empty cottages, some tumbling down. Even the stone ones are without roofs."

I looked over when there was not reply for a few moments. Thomas's jaw was tight, and his face held a dark countenance.

"What you're seeing is the high price of fighting for freedom," he said between clenched teeth. "The famine we have all heard about has barely touched us in Kinsale, or Corke, or even Galway, compared to the smaller villages throughout Ireland. I know you are aware armies come through, take all they want, and burn the rest to the ground. The farmers who barely live through the winter have always had to count on the spring and summer crops to survive. It only takes one season without for them to suffer starvation." And it's not just the English, our own Chieftains do the same to feed themselves and then destroy to deny the enemy any food which may remain. Tis a terrible thing and it's those who have the least who suffer the most. As you can now see, hearing about it and seeing it are two different things"

"Well," I thought out loud. "Surely they could find something to eat and why would they abandon their homes? They certainly would still need the shelter."

"Darlin', that's the ultimate cruelty of it. These people don't own their land or their homes. They farm for a landlord and pay them out of their harvest for the rent and the use of the cottage. When they have no harvest, the landlords force them out. Even before eviction might happen, the bastards who burnt their crops also take anything of value, destroy the home and turn them out into the cold. Fiona, these families are literally starving to death. They are reduced to eating grass and nettles, but it only puts something in their stomachs, but nothing they can live on. Parents kill their children when they see they are so weak they won't survive, and they don't want them to suffer any more. There have even been stories of the living surviving by eating the dead. The lucky ones may have family they can go to who aren't as badly off. You'll see less of this as we get closer to Galway for at least there one can find churches and others who are Christian enough to provide some sustenance to these wandering families."

My heart broke to hear such horror and I felt tears on my face, but there was nothing I could say. I closed my eyes and prayed, for this was beyond the common man's ability to change, or to even understand the unfairness of it. When we stopped later for a rest and a bite of bread and cheese, I was as grateful for it as I would have been for a grand feast.

Near the end of our third day I noticed the ground was becoming mostly rough and rocky. More and more stony outcroppings of limestone appeared and there were almost no trees, most certainly none of significant size. The land looked dry and parched and the only streams we saw were more like rivulets.

"Thomas? Does this land always look this way? I see what appear to be farms, but I can't imagine a family could grow enough to survive."

"Ah! We've entered the northern section of County Clare. This area is called the Burren. In the Irish, it's Boireann meaning Great Rocks. It usually does look like this year-round but more colorful when the gorse and wildflowers come in. Surprisingly it's a good place to raise cattle. A rich and nourishing grass grows well in clumps between rocks. Look over to east. You'll see a wee herd right there!"

"Oh my! I see them and they do look fat and healthy. What I wouldn't give to be able to pick them up and set them down in Kinsale. We have hills covered in grass and hardly a cow to be seen now and here it seems they thrive on rock!"

"There aren't as many cows as there used to be, but the farmers work together to protect the ones they have from theft. And, for whatever reason, the climate is milder here which is a great benefit to the farmers."

As I felt a frigid wind numbing my face and pulling at my cloak, I decided I would just have to take his word for it.

I slept leaning against Thomas's shoulder and dreamed we would be on this journey forever. I knew as exhausted as I was, Thomas had to be more so. As we traveled north, the fare at the inns became more and more meagre and Thomas was asleep as soon as he lay down. He had no time to rest during the trip, as I did. I told him I would take the reins, but he wouldn't hear of it. He said there was always a chance the horse would be spooked, and I wouldn't have the strength to control it. I awoke and thought I was home. I could even smell the sea and the jostling of the wagon finally stopped.

"Fi? Darlin', wake up and take a look."

We were stopped on a hilltop and in the distance was a huge stretch of water with numerous rocky islands and fingers of land reaching out into the bay. I thought the inlet at Kinsale was large, but it was nothing compared to the enormous expanse laid before me. The silvery streaks of water between the wedges of land grew further and further apart until I saw nothing but a never-ending mirror which was the bay.

Hugging me close, Thomas said, "Were almost there Fiona. About two hours and we'll be in Galway itself."

"How much further from Galway is the Lynch castle?"

Smiling, he explained, "It's right in Galway, not too far from the quay. Even though it's a castle, it's tied to the sea, not to the land!"

My fatigue disappeared and I could hardly wait to arrive. As we got closer, Thomas pointed out the protective wall around Galway.

"A bit more impressive than the one around Kinsale, aye? It's very thick and just a few years ago they added another arch for entering the city. It's been said Christopher Columbus came to Galway in the 1470's and prayed at St. Nicholas church before a voyage. Ha, you'll be walking on the same stones as the man who discovered the Americas!"

I wasn't sure what struck me the most after entering Galway itself! After the narrow winding streets at home I was pleased to see how wide they were here. Not only could the people easily walk two by two, there was even room for carriages at the same time. It was a busy town and once we entered Shop street, I could see it was aptly named. There were so many different types of merchants, including many public houses. The smells coming from them made my mouth water and reminded me it had been a long time since Thomas, and I had stopped and finished off the last of our bread. The cheese had disappeared the day before.

"There it is, Fiona. We've finally arrived."

Thomas was pointing to a large, square limestone building sitting at the corner of Shop Street and what I was to find out was Abbeygate Rd. It was four stories high with lovely large windows on the second and third floors. Its entry was just to the left of center opening right onto Shop street! Looking up I noticed rain spouts protruding and much to my surprise, they looked like some kind of monsters. I pointed them out to Thomas, and he said they were called gargoyles and were quite common in England and Europe. Personally, I thought they were a bit gruesome and I preferred the simpler clay spouts we had at home. Many of the windows had carved moldings and there were also several different Coats of Arms carved onto the walls. I assumed the one over the door was the Lynch's, but Thomas had to tell me about the others. One represented King Henry VII and another was from the Fitzgeralds of Kildare. I knew the Lynch's were important, but I had no idea they were so connected. For them to personally ask for Thomas to work for them and to offer to take us in, was almost beyond my ken.

We identified ourselves to the servant answering the door. "Ah, sure and you were expected. Please follow me."

As plain as the exterior was, the interior was lovely. There were flowers on the huge table in the entry, and where they got them this time of year was beyond me. There were already some greenery and ribbons on display for the upcoming Christmas celebrations. With all the events and turmoil which was going on in Kinsale and our move, I had forgotten about Christmas.

Exquisite tapestries hung on the walls and a fireplace was keeping the damp chill at bay. We were led to a smaller sitting room which was equally pleasing and had several seating areas placed about. The servant, Titus, as he introduced himself, told us the Lady Lynch would be with us shortly and we were to feel free to partake of the fare laid out and a choice of spirits. We did so, most gratefully, but chose to sit on the un-upholstered chairs due to the condition of our traveling clothes. The room had a most interesting floor of white and black marble squares. "Why, it looks just like a huge chessboard!" I exclaimed. "Wouldn't it be fun to play a game on it?" Thomas agreed, then he pointed out the tapestry opposite the large window. "I would guess this tapestry was hung here to catch the indirect light from the window. It would be worthy of the effort. Look at the colors and details."

He was right! It was obviously a hunting scene, but the realistic figures and action almost came to life. The greens were not just green, they were an assortment of different shades giving the trees a marvelous depth. The stag's eyes were rolling back and showing white as he realized his plight. The hunters were all dressed in a myriad of hunting tunics and they all carried spears, or crossbows. I could almost hear the shouts of excitement as they closed in on their prey. I had could have stared at this marvelous work of art for hours!

We sensed the door open and a melodious voice said, "Welcome to our home! I'm Lady Lynch. My husband Christopher, Lord Lynch should be home from the office soon. I trust your journey was uneventful."

Lady Lynch was as lovely as she was courteous. Tall and well formed with rich reddish-brown hair piled up in a fetching fashion, yet properly covered by a kerchief. However, the kerchief was made of an exquisite lace with ivory silk ties hanging down. I had never seen such a large piece of lace before. The most I'd seen was on the edge of a handkerchief, or a bit added to a collar. Thomas immediately bowed with his leg stretched forward, with such grace I was most proud. I curtseyed as we gave our thanks for their generosity and apologized for our rather disreputable appearance. Lady Lynch smiled in a most welcoming manner and said to not be concerned. She assured us her staff had taken care of our horse and wagon. However, they told her they were concerned because they could find no satchels, or bags, to take up to our quarters. Thomas explained the hidden compartment and the trick to opening it. She found the feature to be delightfully clever and passed the message on to Titus to tell the footman. With that, Lord Lynch entered and greeted us. He was handsome with dark hair a bit longer than the close-cut current fashion. This was to his advantage for the white wings at his temple gave him a dramatic flair. I could tell immediately he was a man of energy and action and his eyes sparkled with intelligence and humor. He and his wife both put us at ease.

The footman, James, entered, and Milord said he would show us to our rooms where we were to freshen up and rest a bit before supper. We were instructed to ring for assistance should we require anything.

We followed James in a bit of a daze and entered our room. I should say 'our rooms' We had a bedroom with two upholstered chairs by the window, a chest, a privacy screen, and huge bed which looked as soft as a cloud. Through an open door I could see a sitting room with a beautiful desk. Thomas's eyes lit up at such a luxury. No more cramped little corner with one candle. Both rooms already had fires laid and burning.

Wrapping his arms around me, Thomas whispered in my ear, "Well, Mrs. Lydon, I believe we have entered a magic land of adventure! Are you willin' to share it with me?"

As much as I wanted to just crawl into such a lovely bed and sleep, we took advantage of the ewer of hot water, cloths and a pot of scented soap. By the time we were done, we had transferred an amazing amount of grime from us to the water basin! We also worked at getting our clothes in a bit better condition as our baggage had not been brought up yet. Just about the time we were done with our cleanup and dressed, a servant arrived who came to escort us downstairs for a lovely meal.

After we dined, we were invited to join our hosts in the sitting room. While we enjoyed a drink and the Lord described some of Thomas's new duties, I looked out the window and saw the drizzle of the grey, raw day had turned to snow. The soft flakes swirled about and I felt them to be a sign we would be blanketed in safety and hospitality here.

WINTER 1601 - GALWAY

A tentative tapping at the door awakened me and I could tell by the light through the window the sun had been up awhile. A young girl, about thirteen, in a brown dress and white apron, entered and curtsied. She carried a fresh basin of steaming water.

"Sure, and I'm sorry to be disturbin' you ma'am, but milady said I should be doin' for you while yer here. Me name's Rosie"

"Well good morning Rosie. I'm Mrs. Lydon. I don't think I'll be needing much doing though."

Apparently, this flustered her a bit as her faced turned a tad red and she stammered out, "I'd be glad to brush out yer hair, if it would be alright?"

Her eyes darted around, and she spotted my cloak, which she grabbed and held up for me to use as a robe. Smiling, I accepted this gesture, which seemed to put her at ease. Not being used to having a lady's maid, I was also not used to conducting my morning ablutions in front of strangers. I asked her if she would be kind enough to give me a few private moments and upon her return, I would be pleased to have her do my hair. After she left, I dug around and was relieved to see my good clothes had traveled well. I laid them out thinking how nice it would be to wear something besides our traveling clothes! I then used the most welcome hot water. By the time Rosie returned I felt fully refreshed. It was a wonderful indulgence to have her brush my hair and put it up to fit under my cap.

Smiling shyly at my obvious pleasure she said, "Milady asked if you would be kind enough to join her in the sunroom when you be ready. I'll take ye there and then bring you a wee bite and tankard, if ye wish."

"That would be grand! Let's go now and not keep Lady Lynch waiting."

Rosie led me down one flight of stairs to a delightful little room which had a window which not only got the morning sun, it was high enough to probably get sunlight most of the day. There were even some window boxes holding a few hardy flowers which were likely to become a bright display once the winter was over. The lady of the house was seated at a lovely little desk with clever slots and openings for paper, ink and pens.

She looked up from her work and gave me a warm smile. "Good morning, my dear. I trust you slept well after your long journey. Thomas seemed full of energy and ready to start the day! He's a dear and hardly looks a day older than when he was studying in Glasgow. He came to supper frequently and by the soundness of his appetite, we could tell the lad needed it."

"Yes. I felt as though I was sleeping on air! Your kindness is most appreciated, Lady Lynch."

"Oh please, do call me Moira, if I might also call you Fiona. I would feel so much more comfortable being able to be less formal while at home. The continual 'Lord' and 'Lady' can get quite tiresome. Rosie is bringing you some breakfast and I was hoping we could take this time to talk about your time here. I know Thomas will be a great help to Christopher. More and more shipping is coming into Galway as it seems to be the safest port during all of this upheaval. Much of it is from foreign countries and Thomas's fluency in those other languages, as well as Latin and the Irish, will be invaluable."

"Thank you Mi'lady, er, Moira. I know he is quite excited about the opportunity. He loves a challenge and has no fear of hard work! I don't imagine the Lord counted on me being part of the offer and I certainly hope I can be of some help to you while I'm here. Thomas was quite leery of leaving me in Kinsale during this siege."

"Oh Fiona! We wouldn't have it any other way. Besides, I doubt he would be able to fully concentrate on his duties here if he knew his wife and babe were in danger!"

I could feel the color rise in my cheeks and she quickly exclaimed, "Dear me. Thomas told me you were expecting. I don't mean to embarrass you. I think it's delightful. I've no surviving daughters of my own, so I look forward to being somewhat involved in the process. I hope you don't mind."

Tears sprang to my eyes. "Not at all Moira. With my mother so far away, it would be a blessing to have another woman to turn to."

"I am most pleased! Ah, here's she is with a bite to eat. Please enjoy while I finish this correspondence. Since the weather appears to be clearing, let me take you for a carriage ride this afternoon and show you our neighborhood."

By the time we left it was chilly, but the sun was out. We were also bundled up with wool blankets and lap rugs. Moira took us around the corner and onto Shop Street. At the next corner she showed me St Nicholas Church where we would be attending services on Sundays. It was much larger than St. Multose and she said it was almost four hundred years old.

"It's beautifully made. I see some scaffolding on one side. Are they doing some repairs?"

Smiling, Moira proudly said, "No. The Lynches are going to add an entire new section on one side and the Ffrench family immediately jumped in and pledged the same for the other side. Instead of the typical rectangular shape, St. Nicholas will be square with three peaks! We are truly blessed to be able to do this as Galway has grown much and there is barely room to squeeze in during services! Hopefully the initial plans for the stained-glass window will be considered while you are here. Wouldn't it be wonderful for you to help us choose the designs?"

I let her know how pleased I was at such a prospect as she instructed her driver where to go next.

"I'm going to take us to the quay. You should see where your husband will be spending his days and the scope of his responsibilities. Be sure to bundle up. The breeze off the bay can be bitter cold. When we have nicer days, I may have you accompany Rosie when she shops so you will learn what's in our community. For example, we have the most wonderful baker just around the corner. Our cook handles most of our basic needs, but Nicholas is a genius with pastries and fancy cakes. There are mornings, when the wind is right, where the aromas from his ovens will make your mouth water!"

As promised, the winds grew stronger and cold as we got closer to the docks, I could truly smell the sea instead of the rather noisome odors of the crowded town. I felt invigorated and was enjoying our little adventure. The first thing I noticed was the wall around Galway. I had seen them at a distance, but now I realized how very thick and tall they were. I understood why the Spanish were concerned about Kinsale's wall. They looked like a child's fort compared to Galway's ramparts. The newest arch at the end of the old wall was at least 40 paces deep. As we drove through it, the view of the ships and the bay spread out before us. There were so many vessels coming, going and at anchor I couldn't even count them. Numerous buildings and warehouses lined the docks, and all was a hustle and bustle of color, languages and movement. Kinsale was a safe and pleasant harbour, however, not one tenth of the commerce I saw here could have been handled back home.

Moira had the driver pull up to a weathered, but sturdy building. There we were let out and Moira took me through the main door. By the immediate attention and greeting she received, I could tell she was much respected. She asked that her husband and his new assistant be advised of our presence and we were escorted to a small, but cozy room decorated with wonderful paintings of ships at sea and a collection of shipboard instruments including some which were a mystery to me.

A pleasant fire was going and there was comfortable seating. Within a short while, Lord Lynch and Thomas entered the room. Thomas greeted me with a huge smile and a heartfelt hug. Lord Lynch also greeted Moira quite warmly and was obviously glad to see her.

"Well, well. What a wonderful surprise and a great excuse for a little refreshment".
The Lord rang a bell and a young man entered.

"O'Connell do bring us some ale, cheese and those biscuits of which I'm so fond. There's a good lad."

Turning to me, "I would imagine Moira wanted to come down to be sure I was treating your man kindly and so you could be assured all was well. She's quite the mother hen when it comes to such things,"

"She has been most kind my Lord. I am quite taken by the immense amount of activity going on. I don't know how you keep track of it all."

Lord Lynch chuckled and said, "Fortunately I only have to keep track of part of it. There are many, many merchants who use Galway. The wine trade itself is huge, and even more so now the ports to the south are deemed to be in jeopardy. In fact, it's the reason I asked for Thomas' help!"

Addressing Thomas, Moira asked, "And how goes your first day Thomas. I trust Christopher isn't overwhelming you."

"Ah well, it is a lot more than I am used to, but I find it quite exciting! I have already learned some shortcuts from some of the other clerks which make the tasks easier and yet more accurate. I am also feeling some of the rust falling away from my language skills. I had limited need of them in Kinsale, for most of the manifests, etc. were quite repetitious. But here there is much more detailed correspondence in French, Italian, the Irish and even Dutch!"

I had to smile at the sparkle in his eyes.

Facing her husband, Lady Lynch said "I trust you are being kind. You tend to think your clerks should work as fast and know as much as it took you to learn in thirty years!"

Christopher smiled and responded, "Well, Moira, on top of his keenness for numbers, experience in working for his father-in-law, an understanding of sailing, languages plus enthusiasm, you may see me home much earlier in the near future. On the other hand, Fiona, I fear your husband will be getting in later and barely have time to sup before cavorting in the arms of Morpheus, leaving any long conversations for Sundays!"

Within short order our days took on a new, yet comfortable pace. Moira had decided to take me under her wing and introduce me some ladies in her social circles and, in so doing, make me a little more aware of current etiquette. Galway was definitely more 'English' in politics, social order and opinions than Kinsale. Moira felt, should Thomas become more involved and proficient in the business, we should also be more aware of how to act around those whom Thomas would depend for his reputation. I wrote to my family as often as I could and had gotten a couple of most appreciated letters in return. In fact, Thomas also heard from Da that The Irish were finally well ensconced above Kinsale but seemed somewhat scattered and at odds as to how to commence anything more than skirmishes. Conditions in and out of town were deteriorating.

One evening Thomas and I were relaxing in our rooms before bed, with me standing before the metal mirror as I brushed my hair. I stood sideways to see if there was any roundness to my stomach. Thomas came up behind me and placed his warm hands on the slightest hint of a bulge.

'I have to admit, I'm quite fascinated by this process and I find it makes you even more desirable to me."

Still behind me, he nuzzled my neck and his hands moved to my shoulders and slowly slid my bed gown down my shoulders, widening the gap in front. He then placed his palms under my now exposed breasts, stroking the nipples with his thumbs while I felt my knees weaken with pleasure.

"I can see and feel the increased fullness which gives you an even more womanly beauty to your figure."

His arousal was apparent by the pressure I felt against my backside. Slowly turning me around he pressed his face between my enlarged breasts, then sliding down to his knees, lovingly pressed his face against my stomach and kissed the mound which held the child. In one movement he lifted me and carried me to our bed and proved quite convincingly his new job did not tire him completely.

The next week was filled with joy and laughter as we finished the preparations for Christmas. Moira had decided, rather than indulging in gift giving, other than the help's expected bonuses, extra alms would be given to charities who were trying to feed the starving and homeless wretches who were victims of the famine. Thomas had given me some of his salary to send home to help those in need in Kinsale too. Mother had said the town's children were suffering fiercely due to the exorbitant price of any kind of fresh milk and vegetables.

December 24th dawned with the city covered in a fresh snowfall which erased soot and refuse and made Galway into a wonderland. Lord Lynch had declared half day's work and Thomas threw a snowball at me with a large laugh as they hurried to get the morning's duties done. Moira and I scurried about keeping the help in line as they prepared our Christmas feast. The Lynches had a tradition of having their festive meal on Christmas Eve so their help could be home, or to at least simply take some ease on Christmas Day. We would all spend Christmas Eve day casually and rest up for the expected rounds to the Lynch's friends the next day, offering good cheer and sweets. The morning went swiftly and smells from the kitchen were heavenly. We could tell both of our men felt the same way by the smiles overtaking them upon entering the door about mid-day. We had a light meal prepared for them in advance to keep them from laying into the prepared food in the kitchen!

With a comforting fire, spiced drinks and good conversation, we were all in very congenial spirits by the time our delightful supper was served. Moira gave the help lovely little baskets of dried fruits to share with their families and friends and I even played a Christmas tune on the lyre which Moira had taught me. They were all most kind in their applause and Moira then displayed her fine musical skill and voice as we joined in.

"Aha!" exclaimed Lord Lynch, "I nearly forgot. A package came for you Fiona in today's post. Unfortunately, I was so excited to bring it to you that I forgot the rest of the correspondence on my desk. I'll dash down and pick it up tomorrow. But we must allow you to open your package tonight!"

This was exciting indeed. I had never gotten a package in the post before and I felt my face warm at being the center of attention. I could tell right away it was from Mam, as her lettering was large and somewhat childish. However, it was as beautiful to me as a piece of art. The package was small and tied with a length of yarn I recognized as made by her own hand. Inside was a set of three small handkerchiefs of white linen on which she had worked embroideries of flowers and each was monogrammed with my new initials. They were exquisite and I instinctively held them to my nose to get a scent of her. Da had enclosed a note and I asked Thomas to read it to me as my eyes were blurred with tears.

"Dearest Daughter: Since your mother didn't have enough time to add to your trousseau, she is hoping these kerchiefs will suffice until such time as the world is an easier place and you will be home. I will divulge a little secret that her efforts now are all on necessaries for your wee one! We miss you most sincerely and your Mam says she now sees what a grand help you were, especially with your little sisters. However, Chloe is rather enjoying her senior status over Katy and I cannot say our Katy is any too pleased with the arrangement. It is a great relief to us that you, Thomas and the babe are out of danger and being well cared for. Be sure to thank the Lord and Lady again for their kindness, should I inadvertently forget to do so in my next correspondence to them. I'm afraid my letters to him are dull fare and we tend to get bogged down in business. Oh yes, also tell Thomas he is sorely missed too. Robbie and Colum are doing their best, but Colum's writing bears a strong resemblance to hen's scratching, but he seems to have a great mind for details.

Robbie's hand is passible, but I fear he would leave his head lying about was it not attached! I suppose this means I will need to keep them both to equal the one. On a more serious note, keeping them busy at the office is a good thing as young men who are seen to be unemployed are now being compelled to join the Spanish troops in defense of the city. I am Irish to the bone but have no wish to see any of my children put in harm's way if it can be prevented.

Molly has come down with a fearsome cough and has not been strong enough to work. Your Mam has insisted she go home so her mother can care for her. Chloe has taken over many of her duties and is a good helper. Your Mother says she seems to have a knack for finding all kinds of bits and pieces which can be added to our meals to make them stretch further and make them more interesting. We're existing much on a steady diet of soups now. However, we have been keeping one of our few chickens better fed than the others as it is destined for our Christmas supper! The boys are making Katy a wee bed for her dolls and we're hoping this will cheer her up. She's not been her usual impish self the last couple of days. The weather is miserable, and we think she is missing you and just doesn't understand why you are so far away.

Love and constant prayers we shall all be together again soon. Your Mam, and Da."

I was torn between the joy of hearing from them, the sadness of knowing their lives were such a challenge now and feeling guilty because we were safe and well-fed. I turned to Thomas and asked if we could purchase a few items, such as salt, oats and dried vegetables, and send them on the next ship stopping there. Pulling me close and kissing my forehead, he said I was to do some shopping after the Holiday, and he would see to it.

Christmas Day 1601 dawned crisp and cold, but clear. We all went to Mass together and it was quite festive with the church festooned with greenery and ribbons. The larger than usual attendance also helped to warm the usually chilly church. My family was much on my mind and in my prayers during the service. After, we hurried home to have some breakfast and celebrate with some music and storytelling. We enjoyed some delightful apple, currant and spice tarts and sausage before I hurried up to my room to retrieve some gifts I had purchased by saving bits of the spending money Thomas had been giving me.

It felt good to be able to give Moira the beautiful aqua ribbons which would perfectly compliment her color and to give Lord Christopher a special glass made to be held over writing, or an object and make it appear larger! They both seemed quite appreciative and each gave me a hug. I then gave Thomas a boxed set of exquisite quill pens and it included a bottle of India ink. I wouldn't normally have been able to afford such a gift, but the box was slightly damaged on one corner and the shop keeper was willing to strike a bargain with me. I must admit a bit of flirting went a long way in winning his generosity. Thomas's eyes sparkled when he opened his gift. I was especially glad when he whispered to me this was the first personal Christmas gift he had gotten since his parents passed away. Not to be outdone, he opened a silken pouch and placed a delicate silver chain with a cross around my neck. He then kissed the nape where it was still warm from his touch while he secured the clasp. I felt tears as I realized how fortunate I was and how badly I felt to have taken advantage of this good man to hide my shame.

Lord Christopher rose and gave a toast with wishes for the troubles to be over before next Christmas and we would all remain in good health to see such a blessing. He announced he would go to the office to pick up the post he had left there as he was expecting some important correspondence. Moira asked him not to dawdle as she and I would be wrapping the little rum-cakes we would all deliver on our Christmas visits upon his return. The time flew by and the Lord was back before we knew it.

He started shuffling through the packets as we donned our cloaks and hats. As I was just preparing to tie my hat's ribbons when he exclaimed,
"What ho! Fiona, here's a letter from your parents. It must be of some import for them to write this so soon after sending your package. Would you like to read it now? We'll be glad to wait."
"Oh yes! Thank you."
As I unfolded the paper, I noted this was written about a week ago which was about a week after my Christmas package had been sent.
"Dearest Fiona: I am penning this for your Mother as I fear she would not be able to do so. I trust Thomas is with you as you read my letter. It is my grievous task to tell you wee Katy was taken from us and now rests with Aileen in the church yard. The illness came on her unexpectedly, but with a fury which gave us no time to hope for recovery. At least the end was without suffering as she was no longer aware of her surroundings. We cling to the memory of seeing her open her eyes and smile, looking toward Heaven as she took her final breaths. It is our belief the angels were there to welcome

her. I know this is a fearsome thing to share when there is no way you can be here to grieve with us, or comfort your Mother, but we know you will say your goodbyes through your heart and your prayers. I also ask you pray for all of us as our home is dark with sadness and we walk about as strangers in a foreign land. It seems losing one child not only does not make it easier to bear losing another, I believe it makes it twice as difficult. Write when you can for it will do your Mother and me a world of good to hear from you and know you are safe.

PostScript: The battles in Kinsale are not going well for the Irish, but not for lack of effort. I think we will know the way of it fairly soon!"

My bonnet slipped unbeknownst from my hand and Thomas looked at me with alarm as the color drained from my face. I reached for him as I started to sway. I felt as cold as dear Katy must be and knew I had to sit. Thomas got to me in time and led me to a chair. Looking at him in despair, I simply held the letter out to him for no words would come to my icy lips. He read the letter aloud and the others were as stunned as I. Sympathy and soothing sounds were being spoken, but I was in a trance. I could hear, but not understand. I could see, but not respond. I suddenly stood and said, sounding as though nothing of import had happened,

"Excuse me. I think I will go upstairs and lay down for a while."

The three of them looked perplexed as I turned and did just that.

"Oh Thomas, we are so sorry for Fiona and her family," Moira said with tears in her eyes, for she had also lost two children. "However, Fiona has been dealt a serious blow and seems not to know how to cope. Christopher and I will make our rounds and be quick about it as this is news which does not need to be shared when others are festive. I think it best you be with her when the reality strikes her for, she will be in need of comfort, patience and understanding."

"Of course. As bereft as I am for Fiona, I too am devastated for Katy was a darling child and the light of their household. This will be most fearsome for Fiona."

I could hear the Lord and Lady Lynch leave and Thomas's tread on the stairs was heavy as he slowly approached our rooms. He found me seated in my chair by the window with my sewing basket on my lap. I had a ball of dark green yarn in my hands and was slowly wrapping the strand round and round my hand. Thomas came and stood in front of me until I looked up with a slight smile as I explained green was Katy's favorite color as it brought out the green in her eyes. Thomas pulled a footstool over and sat with me watching as I tried to cope with this terrible information.

I suddenly stated, "She will be five in September. I promised her I would teach her to read when she turned five." With a quizzical look, I asked him, "How can I teach her now if she's not there?"

Thomas placed his hand on my knee and a moment later, the ball of yarn fell to the floor and I placed my hands to my face and let out a sob which was like to break Thomas's heart. The tears flowed so fast my hands could not stem them. The sobs shook me so hard Thomas felt he must hold me, or I would surely come apart. When the spasms subsided a bit, he picked me up and laid me on our bed. Lying next to me, he offered what comfort he could. Eventually the fatigue brought on by grief finally overtook me. Just as I dropped off into blessed oblivion, I mumbled words which would have made no sense at all to Thomas.

"It's my fault. God is angry with me."

For the next two days, I stayed in bed and could not be coaxed to eat more than a little bread and water. On the third day Thomas came up and told me a ship was leaving for Kinsale this afternoon and if I wished to write Mother and Father, he would see to its dispatch immediately. I looked at him with no comprehension for a moment. He might as well have asked me to walk to Dublin. It was a task which seemed beyond my abilities. I simply bade him,

"Would you write it for me Thomas? I don't know what to say."

With that, I simply rolled over and closed my eyes again, seeking blessed sleep   He quietly went to the desk and composed a letter of the love, heartbreak and sympathy we felt. He didn't tell them of my lethargic condition as the Gearaghty's needed no more grief or worries than they were currently bearing. He sent Rosie out with a list of some non-perishable foods to purchase and made sure they were sent with the letter packet.

Time passed and I was unaware of whether it snowed, or the sun shone. I eventually felt compelled to rise. I got dressed, but walked the house as a wraith, engaging with others only when necessary. Just the effort of responding to a question seemed to be difficult. Moira used her natural warmth to entice me to talk and be tempted with a tasty tidbit, but I would only thank her quietly and walk away. By now the news had gotten to us, after some terrible battles on, and around, Christmas day, the Irish dispersed, and the Spanish surrendered to Lord Mountjoy in Kinsale. What would turn out to be the main and decisive battle for Irish independence in 1601 was over.

I heard the details but wasn't even affected by the news. These events meant as little to me as if they were taking place on the moon. What did any of it mean when so many people suffered, and even innocent children died.

After the New Year, Lord Christopher asked Thomas if he might call a physician to examine me as I was so pale and thin. Thomas agreed with gratitude and the gentleman arrived the next morning. I didn't care one way or the other as he examined and bled me. Speaking with Thomas and the Lynches privately, he said I was suffering from a deep melancholy and told them I would speak of little to him, but especially would not discuss Katy's death.

"She seems to understand completely her sister died of a virulent illness, but for some reason seems to think it was her fault. When I asked her how this could be, she told me, "God is not all forgiveness, He is also a vengeful God.""

"Unless you know of a burden she carries, it is a mystery to me why she feels this way. I am not a priest, so I can only treat her body, not her soul. I recommend you use your status, as her husband, to insist she eats, if not for her sake, then for the sake of the child she bears. She should be fed a small portion of raw calf's liver, every day for at least a week, a cup of milk daily and a fair portion of ale, at least three times a day. I have bled her to release whatever ill humours are in her. When her strength improves, a brief outing each day, weather permitting, should be strongly encouraged. Beyond this, only your kindness and prayers will bring her out of the darkness in which she hides. "

They all thanked him profusely and promised to follow his directions. The kitchen maid was sent out directly to obtain liver from the butcher.

As I sat in our room, the sewing I had picked up a while ago, lay idly on my lap, I kept thinking I had to confess to Thomas. I had to tell him of my deception. Only then would Katy be returned to us. Surely God would forgive me and let her death be merely an awful dream. She would awaken and she would run to Mam's arms asking for her bread and jam. Tears sprang to my eyes as my mind told me I was wrong. Nothing would change. God would work no miracles for me. For the next week I was plied with nourishing foods and kindness. I ate only enough to appease them and went about the household, helping where I could, out of gratitude.

One Saturday morning, Thomas entered the bedroom in a flurry of energy. "Fiona! Get dressed in something warm, bring your gloves and furred bonnet and meet me downstairs." he demanded. "It's a sunny day with barely a breeze and I'm taking you for a ride."

Immediately turning on his heel, he left the room while I still sat there with my mouth hanging open. It was so unlike him to order me about thus I simply did as he asked. He met me at the front door, carrying a large blanket and a basket, and escorted me to the waiting cart. When we were seated, he looked at me for a moment and without a word, put his arm about me and gave me a warm kiss on the cheek, clucked at the horse and we were off.

"Where are we going to Thomas and what's in the basket? I honestly don't feel like visiting."

"Not to worry, my love. I feel we are way overdue for some special time together, so we are going west to Salt Hill for a picnic. The clean sea air and wonderful view of the bay will do us both good."

I could see he was right as we left the noise, odors, and busy streets of Galway. The white clouds held no threat of rain as they played hide and seek with the sun and the sea grasses rustled soothingly as they swayed along the water's edge. I could feel my spirits brighten and Thomas looked more relaxed too as I started to comment on the sights. We soon arrived, and Thomas drove us up to a broken stone wall which, at one time, may have been a crofter's cottage. There we were out of the chilly sea breeze and the sun-warmed stones made a cozy corner for our outing. We spread the woolen blanket out and Thomas gathered some rocks to weight the corners while I brought the basket over. It was only a brief uphill walk from the cart to where we had settled the blanket, but my breath came fast, and I could feel a weakness in my legs. I hadn't realized the effects of my slow decline.

Leaning over my shoulder, he asked "Should we peek and see what the cook put together for us. My stomach is telling me breakfast was quite a while ago."

I laughed as his desire and ability to eat as much and as often as possible, without putting on a bit of fat, had already become a household jest. We found flasks of spiced ale cleverly wrapped in several layers of cloth to keep it warm, some meat pies, a small round of cheese, dried apples and currants plus lovely little cakes with jam. Seeing and smelling this delightful spread of treats, and breathing in the crisp sea air, my appetite flooded back with a vengeance. I could hardly wait to set to! There was no hesitation from my husband and we both attacked the food with an ardor. It was good to feel a need for anything. The world had meant nothing to me in the last three weeks since Christmas. Thomas laughed with joy as I beat him in taking the last cake. When done we fell back on the blanket and groaned with the pleasure of being well filled? Thomas pulled me close and placed my head on his shoulder. Putting his hand on my stomach, he whispered in my ear.

"Now, here's the problem Love. Is this sweet roundness I feel due to the babe makin' its presence known, or due to you eating enough for a starvin' sailor?"

"I would have to say both Thomas. However, I believe the time has come where there will be no doubt to anyone with eyes that I am expecting a child. I hope you have the kindness to still love me when I look more like a milk cow than a wife!"

"I shall force myself somehow" he said with a drowsy smile.

The winter sun, the grand meal and the cozy stone corner soon did their work and we slept in each other's arms for almost an hour.

I woke before Thomas and while lying there, I could feel the darkness pushing its way into my thoughts again. I didn't want to crawl back into the cold blackness but was again feeling my guilty burden was tied to wee Katy's death. Part of me knew this didn't make sense, but I seemed to be unable to let it go. With the comfort of this dear man next to me, I found I could give this dilemma more rational thought than when I was alone in my despair with confusion swirling like a storm at sea. As I turned the facts over in my mind, it slowly occurred to me the one thing I should have done, and didn't, was to confess to my priest. Normally, this would have been the first thing I'd do when feeling troubled or felt I may have committed a sin. However, I had denied myself this Sacrament in Kinsale for our priest knew me, knew all of us well. A servant of God or not, I couldn't face telling him of my shame, nor my deception. The longer I put it off, the more difficult it was until it got to the point of impossible. I couldn't go to the priest in Galway either. He knew the Lynches and he knew we were guests in their home. He also struck me as one of those men who were more interested in politics and gossip rather than tending to parishioners' souls. I needed guidance and could find none. Closing my eyes, I prayed again, for the hundredth time, for Mother Mary's intercession and for God to give me peace and guide me to find an answer for my troubled soul.

Thomas awoke shortly after and we loaded up the cart. I wrapped the blanket around us as the air had taken on a deeper chill and the cloud cover had increased. Thomas chattered about plans at his office and hopes of increased and easier trade now the battle at Kinsale was over and the other skirmishes were inland. Even though the Spanish surrender and the Chieftains' failures were a disappointment there was now a possibility of lives getting back to normal. My answers to his comments were brief as my prayers were foremost in my mind.

Shortly before seeing the gate to Galway, the sun suddenly came out from behind two clouds and shone a brilliant beam of light on a small picturesque building nestled on the hillside.

"Look at how lovely the light is over there. It makes the building shine like a sun. Oh! It's a church. I wonder which one."

"It's a small parish church which serves the families on and around Salt Hill. It's closer for them than going all the way into Galway and I'm sure they feel more comfortable having Mass with friends and family who, undoubtedly, carry different burdens than the parishioners who attend St. Nicholas."

My heart stopped as a thought entered my head as clearly and boldly as if it was written in front of my eyes. I wondered if I could seek a priest there! I would simply be an unknown traveler needing guidance. I could easily get the Lynches' driver to take me while running errands. I didn't think there would be any question as to why I wanted to stop by a church. The family knew I was distraught and would, undoubtedly, welcome any sign I was trying to find my way to peace and acceptance. The afternoon seemed suddenly brighter as I now saw a possible spiritual lifeline.

JANUARY 1602 - GALWAY

No one was sure why I started to come out of my cocoon, but everyone in the household breathed easier now they felt I had come to grips with my Katy's death. To facilitate my plan, I made sure to periodically go on short outings during the day with Titus as my willing coachman. This gave him a chance to get out of his usual household duties and see a bit of the town. A perfect opportunity came one day when the Lord and Lady were both to be gone for a fair amount of time visiting a relative staying nearby. It was a bright day and I asked Titus if he would take me for a ride out toward Salt Hill for the view. He did so, gladly and I made sure to wear one of my older cloaks in order to look less prosperous to the local folk and the priest. I could feel my anxiety building as we got closer to the little parochial church. I kept rehearsing what I would tell the priest so as not to leave out important information and yet not have to go into too much detail. I tried to fix in my mind on the things for which I felt most guilty and the questions I needed to ask to ensure I understood the churches standings on such matters. Hard as I tried, I felt unprepared, but determined, by the time the church came into view.

"Titus," I called out, "Would you be good enough to let me off at this church. I would like to learn more about its history and perhaps speak with the priest. I may be a while. However, I noticed a public house just over there where you might want to take some refreshment."

He couldn't hide his smile at this unexpected suggestion.

"Aye, Milady! I'll sit near the window as I'll be lookin' for you when you come out. You just wait by the entrance and I'll be back to pick you up afore you know it."

Titus left and I took a deep breath before entering the church. As my eyes adjusted to the darkness, I noticed its simplicity. The few furnishings and statues were rustic and simple, but there was a sense of warmth and frequent use to the building. I was disappointed at first for the church appeared empty. Then a slight movement caught my eye and I saw a priest kneeling before the altar in prayer. I waited and after he made the sign of the cross and stood, he noticed me. With a friendly tilt of his head and a bit of a look of surprise, he asked,

"Good day my child. How may I help you?"

I hid a smile at his reference to me as a child since I could see he probably wasn't much older than Thomas.

"Good morning Father. I am in need of spiritual counseling and was wondering if you might have time to hear my confession?"

"That will be no problem. I must admit most of the confessions I hear are on a Saturday after the previous evening revelries, yet in time to make the supplicant acceptable to the Lord at Sunday Mass."

His Leinster accent had a comforting lilt and I followed him to a simple confessional with a threadbare black curtain across it. I could feel my heart beating faster and the sweat on the back of my neck as we approached. It took me a few false starts to tell him my tale, but he was kind and encouraged me to go on. Once I started, the story poured out of me and I couldn't hold back my tears. It was so painful to relive such a vicious assault through the re-telling and then to make it worse, I had to admit to my boldness in enticing Thomas to be intimate with me and of my deception to get him to wed me. I told him why, without mentioning names, or places, I had not confessed this before. I also told him of Katy's death and how I could not help but feel I brought this tragedy down upon my family. Then there was silence.

After a moment, he said,"This has surely been a great burden for you to carry by yourself. I believe the complexity will require we look at these events individually. The first thing you must accept is the terrible deed done to you was of no fault of your own. Sure, and you can't think our Lord would hold it against you. If, as you say, you did nothing to encourage the scoundrel, and you did your best to fight him off. You are a victim of the evil which lives with us in this world, nothing more. Therefore, I would ask you to pray for his soul and ask God to ensure he not have the opportunity, or need, to inflict such an atrocity on any other woman. Do you believe you can do this and release the unfounded guilt within you?"

With a sense of relief, I reassured him I could, with God's help.

"Now, dear child, I can understand your reluctance, embarrassment and fear of telling your parents of this violation. However, this is where you should have trusted God to help you and to have faith your parents would love and support you. This was a problem much larger than you should have tried to resolve on your own. For this, you must ask God's forgiveness for your lack of faith. By failing to trust Him, the following decisions you made have created the additional burdens of guilt which eat at you. Please know I think you did what you felt you must, but as frequently happens, making such choices without God's guidance, only makes it worse. I am reassured you seem to truly care for your husband, and you intend to be a good wife to him. Yours is a most hopeful attitude. However, keep in mind, if you had gone to your parents, they may well have come to the same conclusion in wedding this man, but by being honest with all and without deceit. From what you tell me, he sounds like the type of lad who would have come to your rescue, rather than toss you aside. Do you agree?"

Lowering my head, and feeling the tears falling again, I whispered, 'Yes Father. I can see it now although I know it would have been a humiliating and horrid admission. I have to say I would have lived with the fear that he would have only married me to save me from such a fate, and not for the love he has for me."

"Did you not say he had already asked your father for your hand and he had always shown a deep feeling for yourself and your welfare?"

"Yes! However, I am also thinking of the child. I must admit I have doubts I can look at this child daily without seeing the man who did this and the vile way in which the babe was created. It would be even worse to lay such a burden on an innocent man who is now expected to raise another man's child, let alone love it."

The priest was silent for a long moment, then speaking softly, said, "As for your feelings, you must consider this child as a gift from God. A babe is a blessing no matter how it is conceived. Remember within this child also lies parts of you, your siblings, your parents and their parents. By some mystery, these parts of us live on. I have a cousin who could easily pass for me and he also entered the priesthood. We even have a similar birthmark. Therefore, think upon those qualities in your family in which you can rejoice, and should you see something in your child you feel may be an unwelcome sign of this man, pray on it and do your best to teach and guide your child in the proper ways to live. Keep in mind all children have good and bad in them, even from the best of parents, so yours will not be so different. Can you accept this as truth?"

"Oh Father! You mean there may be hope I might be able to raise and love this babe. If so, it will become part of my morning prayers to the Blessed Virgin."

"Now," his voice becoming a bit stern, "The question of telling your husband of this situation is of utmost importance. As much as I dislike dishonesty, or deceit, I'm not overly concerned if you share this with your parents. I say this because they are dealing with a great loss at this time and could not easily carry this additional burden. They are no longer involved in this as you have already made your decisions, and this is now between you, your husband and God. I suggest you not unburden yourself to your parents and simply grant them the healing they may well receive through this new child. However, there is your deceit in misleading your husband and not telling him the truth of the matter. You not only committed the sin of initiating carnal relations before marriage, you tempted him, on purpose, to do the same. For this, my dear, you are truly in need of God's forgiveness. I am not going to say you must confess to your husband immediately, for my heart tells me you need to speak at length to God to know his will and his timing and He will guide you."

I breathed a sigh of relief for this was not a task I was ready to make right now. This reprieve was yet another blessing, even if only a postponement. This kind and wise priest rendered my penances, which were not light, blessed me after my Act of Contrition and wished me, the babe and my husband a long and loving life. I stayed for a short while in prayer in front of the Virgin Mary and left a donation in the poor box which would probably be considered a welcome addition in this poor parish church. I took an extra moment, or so, to dry my eyes and compose myself before waiting in front of the church. Titus was as good as his word and was there with the carriage in very short order. I'm not sure how long I was with the Father, but it was long enough to have the visit to the Public House put a cheery glow on Titus cheeks and a jaunty song on his lips as he took me back to Galway.

SPRING 1602 - GALWAY

As the weeks passed our daily lives went on in productive and pleasant ways. Thomas was able to take on more responsibility at the office, which kept him at his desk until late, but gave us more to talk about when he got home, and Moira took on a self-appointed task of teaching me new skills. She said she had seen how far a talented and hard-working young man could go in society, even without 'proper' lineage and she anticipated I might need a better introduction to entertaining and etiquette. This was even more important as all signs pointed toward England's greater influence as the Irish were pushed further and further back. She had already been introducing us to people in various levels of society until I was quite comfortable with such soirees and parties. I also was taught it was important to know what subjects could be discussed and those which were best left unsaid. She took me shopping and helped me select some nicer fashions which downplayed my rounding figure and even a couple of hats. The style was narrow and somewhat tall, rather like a pipe and I felt a bit silly in them, but others thought they were the height of fashion. Personally, I still preferred the comfort of a nice white cap, but it was too provincial. I tried to tell her I couldn't accept such generosity, she simply hugged me and said she would do the same for a daughter and had decided to take me on as her own personal project.

I also noticed the Lynch's started entertaining more often at home, and of course Thomas and I were to join in the festivities. We did enjoy such parties and soon learned to identify those who felt superior, those who were harebrained, but didn't know it, and those who were sharp and knowledgeable. The company was stimulating, and an advantage was, in most cases. the men and women conversed and mingled together. Even though our comments regarding what the men were talking about were not taken very seriously by them, at least we got to hear what was going on and then we women could talk about such matters later on our own.

I heard from Mam and Da more frequently and was eased by knowing they were slowly learning to cope with Katy's death. I believed it helped inasmuch as they were both so busy rebuilding Kinsale and working to help the townspeople regain their lives. I know putting off the task of telling Thomas about my secret was also helped by staying so busy here. I imagined some perfect moment in the future which would give me an opening, but not now.

By May, Moira decided a French tutor should be found for me. I tried to explain to her I had little education beyond learning to read, write and cipher and she should not go to such trouble for me.

Chuckling, she said, "My wee bird, learning a language does not depend on formal education. I heard tell even small infants can learn to speak a language!"

It took me a moment before I caught her meaning and I smiled. She chucked me under my chin.

"Fiona, you have been with us long enough for me know you have a sharp and agile mind. I think you will enjoy such lessons very much."

"Thank you for the compliment. However, I don't see the advantage for me speak French. I will be going back to Kinsale in a few months and we live a much more pastoral life there."

"I believe you may be underestimating the benefits of such knowledge. Have you not heard some of our guests make comments in French, let alone converse, and wondered what they said, or responded to such by trying to guess the meaning by context? Also, you must consider as the troubles in Ireland recede, we will all be seeing much more travel and trade. Thomas and you will eventually have your own home and will be entertaining merchants from all over. You will be ever so much more confident if you can converse with your guests and they will go home feeling Ireland is not quite the wild and savage land they thought. There is one more thing to consider. Sharing intimate conversation with your husband can be even more romantic in French! I will leave it up to him to teach you that special vocabulary."

She laughed as my face colored deeply, kissed me on both cheeks and said she thought I was a dear.

Thinking on it, I knew learning French was a good idea and when I told Thomas he was very pleased. He said something in French, then told me it meant I was dearer to him than life itself and he was proud to be the husband of a woman who used her mind. I knew I would do my best to learn such a lovely language.

Friday I was introduced to Jeannette Moreau. She was a petite brunette with a most lush head of hair! She said she had moved to Galway with her husband, a vintner, ten years ago, yet her accent was still quite heavy. She explained she had to teach her now grown children to speak English because they had been raised in France, thereby she was able to learn English herself. According to Lady Lynch, she had been asked by many of the upper class in Galway to teach them French, so came highly recommended. I immediately took a liking to her for she seemed high spirited and her hazel eyes sparkled with humor. She quickly discovered my French was quite limited to not much more than 'merci' and 'bon jour'

"Aha!" she exclaimed, "zees weel be un grand challenge, non? We weel make eet fun and you shall be my finest student. Now, you must understand zees one zing. Ween I come to you on Monday, we weel not speak zee English, nor zee Irish, wheech I do not comprehend at all. We weel learn as zee leetle children learn, non? C'est bon. Eet is settled."

She then spoke briefly to Moira in a French which was so rapid I couldn't determine where one word ended and the next began. I stood there stunned wondering how she could teach me a foreign language without speaking the only language we had in common. As she prepared to leave, she bid me 'au revoir', then looked directly at me until I realized she wanted me to repeat it. I said "Ow ravar" She repeated 'au revoir slowly, looking at me again. I repeated it back, apparently changing the pronunciation to something more acceptable for she smiled broadly and opening the door said, "Oui! And zo we begin."

Thomas found me to be rather jumpy and quiet during the weekend which surprised him as this was normally our time to share and enjoy. But Monday loomed like doomsday to me. I felt Moira would be wasting her money on hiring Jeannette and I would die of shame when it was determined I was simply unteachable. The day finally arrived, and I couldn't even think about eating a bite before the appointed start time of 9:00 a.m. Jeannette arrived and we were settled in the library. She was carrying a rather large satchel, from which she took a sizeable piece of slate and a smaller one, which she gave to me. The larger one she set upright on an easel. She then gave me a piece of white material, like limestone, but finer. She took a similar piece and wrote 'Bon jour' on her slate, said it out loud and pointed to me in such a way I knew she wanted me to duplicate her actions. I was comfortable with that because I knew what Bon jour meant, and I repeated it back to her. Surprisingly, she shook her head, said "Non." and repeated it again slowly. Yes. I could hear a difference. We did this three time before she seemed satisfied. She then said "Je m'appelle Jeannette.", pointing at me to reply.

"Je m'appelle Jeannette." I said. With a light laugh, she said "Non, non! Fiona. Je m'appelle Fiona!"

Oh. Now I saw what she meant. "Je m'appelle Fiona" I responded. We spent the rest of the morning with her drawing objects on her slate, naming them, then writing the word in French. I wrote the same on my slate as we practiced. I learned to concentrate more on memorizing the sounds of the words rather than the written word. I found the spelling difficult to associate with the pronunciation. It was not the same as English. When she left at mid-day, I was exhausted and hoped I would remember some of the words by the time she returned on Wednesday. Fortunately, Moira was gone for several hours and I took a much-needed nap.

Thomas was interested in my first day of lessons when he came home, and I was able to share what I had learned. In fact, I even learned more because I greeted him with Bon Jour, and he explained at night, I would say "Bonne Nuit." I liked this word, nuit. It had a soft round sound to it. I repeated it several times and for some silly reason, it pleased me to learn a new word with Thomas instead of just Jeannette. For several weeks it seemed I was learning many words, but I didn't feel I was 'speaking' French. Suddenly one morning, Jeannette asked me a question and without really thinking about it, I answered her in French. I don't know who was more surprised, her or me. She clapped her hands, reached down and took mine in hers and said "C'est bon Cherie!" The lessons now seemed to fly by, and I could hardly wait for our next session. Thomas spent time with me writing in French when he wasn't too tired, and it helped me even more. By the end of May, my time with Jeannette was at an end and I knew I would miss her. I had much to learn, but I could hold my own with the usual simple chatter at a supper and I had several books I could use to study on my own. The hard part was the pronunciation, especially with my Irish accent and Thomas could help me with it. As we said our goodbyes on our last morning together, Jeannette gave me a small package as a farewell gift. I opened it and it was an exquisite ceramic pin with a painting of the Notre-Dame cathedral in Paris. With tears in my eyes, I hugged her and thanked her for her patience and kindness. I knew I would treasure her gift always.

Thomas chuckled one Sunday morning as he watched me literally roll out of bed.

"Are you sure you're expecting, or have you been having too many ales at the public house. You're startin' to bear a strong resemblance to one of O'Shaughnessy's patrons. Come to think of it, I'm not sure if it's your lumbering gait, or the roundness of the belly." I threatened to throw the chamber pot at him, so he shut up, but he caught my grin and knew he was safe from harm. Coming up behind me, he nuzzled my neck, luxuriating in my unbound hair.

"How is it your hair always smells as sweet as a flower garden and soft as a wee kitten? I sometimes catch myself daydreaming at my desk thinking of your hair!"

I blushed with pleasure at his words, but simply told him I was pleased he thought me more worthy of consideration than a ledger full numbers and cargo.

"Come," he said walking me over to my chair. "we've plenty of time before Mass and I'd like to have a private word with you."

My eyes studied his face, but I saw nothing indicating a problem or concern, even though I could see he had something of import to share.

"All is going well at the office and the Lord Lynch has given me many tasks, over and beyond those needed to care for your father's business. This is not a complaint as he has also paid me quite well to do so and I have learned ever so much. However, I see several changes on the horizon. First, I would have to be blind to not realize summer is not the only thing which will be bursting forth soon! Also, I have, out of expediency, been re-routing more and more of your fathers ships back to Kinsale Harbour as their home port again. It is quite impressive how much more profitable each voyage is when the extra trips to Galway are not necessary. Handling more ships in Kinsale, of course, is also causing more work on his end and although he hasn't pressed the issue, he has hinted he could use my services at home."

I felt my heart beat faster as I realized his meaning. Of course, once the battles abated, I knew we would most likely go home as Thomas promised. But oddly, going home always seemed a long way off and with life being so pleasant here, I had fairly put the thought out of my mind. Suddenly, a rush of homesickness took over.

Grasping his hands, I whispered, "Oh when Thomas, when do you think we may go?"

Laughing, he exclaimed, "Don't hitch up the horse just yet Fiona. It will take some planning to get it done. Which is why I mention it now. We need to prepare as to be ready to go while you're still able to travel. I'll do nothing which will put you in harm's way if I can help it. Your father and I have corresponded several times and he's most anxious for our return and especially to have his darlin' Fi back home. We have decided we will move back into your parent's home, although Colum may not be overly happy having to share a room with Robbie again, but to have you home will make it seem less burdensome. Now, I have saved a fair bit between the Lord's generosity and us not having to pay for lodging all this while. Once we are settled and waiting for the babe to be born, I will be looking for a home we can call our own. How does such a plan sound?"

My heart was singing. A home of our own. It seemed a dream and I couldn't stop myself from immediately starting to plan on setting up housekeeping. I would press Thomas to try to find a place not too far from my parents as I knew my mother needed, now more than ever, to be involved with the babe, as I needed to be close to my mother again. I threw my arms around his neck and hugged him tightly, feeling his morning whiskers on my tear dampened cheeks.

It was decided we would leave Galway in about a month during the first part of June when we would have a chance for warmth and less rain on the journey. Moira was saddened as we made our plans and I assured her I would sorely miss her too. She promised to come to Kinsale herself once the child had survived those most dangerous first months of life and I let her know how much I would love to see her. We thanked them both often during those weeks for all they had done for us and wished we could, in some way repay them their many kindnesses. The month flew by as though it was a week. Our 'wealth' in the form of clothes and material goods had certainly expanded since our arrival a mere five and a half months ago. It also seemed the Lord and Lady Lynch weren't done with their generosity toward us. They had arranged for us to not only have an enclosed and well-appointed coach for the trip home, but also an escort to keep us safe. A new round of tears and hugs started as we prepared to leave and they both told us we were like their own children and Thomas had been an invaluable asset for the Lord's business, as well as my father's. Our trip back to Kinsale was wonderful and we both were able to rest well in the fine coach. The morning of our arrival I was so excited I couldn't keep from peeking out every few minutes for my first sight of the town.

The changes were obvious although the wall had been repaired in quite a few places. However, the lovely green, rolling hills were now scarred and pitted with left-over camp sites and trenches. There was still an unsavory odor about the place, but not as awful as when we left. The harbour, on the other hand, was a beautiful site, filled with ships of all sizes and flags. I could see signs of peace and prosperity coming again to my dear home. We finally reached the house and people started spilling out to greet us. I don't even recall leaving the carriage before I found myself in my mother's arms, with Da right beside her. My brothers were slapping Thomas on the back in boisterous greetings and then the boys turned to the coach with excitement. They both declared it was the finest they'd ever seen and started hinting to Da that this was just what the family needed. Once the emotions settled a bit, Mam had the staff take our staunch escorts inside to offer them refreshments and get them settled so they could get a few days rest before returning to Galway. Knowing my father, he would give them a few coins for their trouble and some gifts for the Lynches.

Chloe had grown considerably and had lost the chubbiness of childhood. Her hair was becoming a thick curtain of burnished gold and it would be her crowning glory. I fully expected to feel Katy barreling into me for a hug before I remembered she was gone. Even during this joyful reunion her absence was tangible. It wasn't until we were all seated and talking over each other like magpies when I noticed both of my parents had aged. They were both thinner; Mam's hair was nearly all gray, and Da's hairline had receded considerably. My brothers on the other hand had changed from boisterous hooligans, to young men, albeit, still somewhat boisterous! I was surprised to see they were quite a handsome pair too. I gave Meg a big hug and could see our previously well-padded housekeeper had lost some weight too. Ma explained Molly had married and then her husband had fallen ill so she had to go home to take care of him. She introduced me to Bridgit, our new kitchen help. She was about my age and lit up the whole room. Her brilliant blue eyes sparkled below a mop of the reddest hair I think I'd ever seen. She had a huge smile and more freckles than stars in the sky. I immediately took a liking to her and Colum informed me she was also, "A right handy cook."

The days passed pleasantly, and I was content to walk about in the gardens and watch as each new flower and herb reached for the warmth of the sun. Mam and I spent lovely mornings in the sewing room. It was such a pleasure to watch her fingers fly as she crocheted lace edging on the babe's gowns. Thomas spent long days at the docks and came home tired and pleased. We had insisted Mam and Da accept a monthly payment as this was only fair and we knew it would help. Da was trying to make up for monies he lost during the war and food, even though available now, was still extremely dear.

By early July I was feeling the babe's growth and was becoming quite uncomfortable with my expanded girth. However, it was also quite pleasant for Thomas and me to lay abed while we both felt the babe kick and shift around. Sometimes it would forcefully straighten an arm, or leg, and create a lop-sided mound which made us giggle. One night, Thomas suddenly raised himself up on his elbow and asked. "Fiona! We haven't seriously discussed a name. It's an important decision, is it not?"

I realized he was right! The birth was getting closer, and even though he and I had mentioned a few names in passing, we really hadn't made any effort to settle on any.

"Well," I suggested, "since most men assume the child will be a son, I suppose we had better start there." We soon found just how many relatives we had once we started trying to incorporate as many as possible into the little one's name. I suggested he be named after Thomas, but he said, "No. Let's save my name for the next."

We finally decided, since this was our first, our parents should be the ones to be honored, so, if a boy, he would be Joseph, after Thomas's late father and Francis, after mine.

"Joseph Francis," I said out loud, "yes, it's a fine strong name. Now wait, you know it could just as easily be a girl!"

"Ah," he sighed, "would you promise she looks just like you? What a delight that would be indeed."

"No promises." I said but couldn't help thinking it was more likely the babe wouldn't look exactly like either of us! More discussion on the subject helped us decide we would still honor Thomas's late father by naming a girl Josephine, and since my mother wasn't fond of Mary (She said it was much too plain) we instantly agreed her middle name should be Kathleen to honor my dear little sister. Thomas leaned down and kissed my very round stomach and whispered, "Good night Joseph, or Josephine. I look forward to meeting you."

Thomas put out some feelers to see what homes might be available in a few months. Unfortunately, there didn't seem to be many. Since some families who had left, had already returned, and more people came as trade had picked up and a semblance of peace had settled over the south. Our population had grown, and empty homes were a rarity. Mam said not to worry as we always had a home with them, and wouldn't it be nice to have help with the babe. I couldn't deny the truth in that, but there was an odd little hunger gnawing at me to have a home of our own. A week, or so later, Thomas announced an agent had contacted him about a home which was vacant and was simply pending some family legal issues needing to be cleared up in about two months.

"Would you like to go see it tomorrow Fi? Mr. Boland, the agent said he could give me the directions in the morning and your Da says there's no problem in leaving the office a wee bit early. We can go look at the house and still be home in plenty of time for supper." My big smile gave him my answer and we all spent the evening trying to discuss this mystery house without a clue to go on! Between the excitement and my physical discomfort, I didn't sleep well, but it seemed a small price to pay for the possibility of seeing our future home.

Mam could tell I was a nervous as a mouse in a room full o' cats in the morning so she gave me a lot of busy work beside my usual tasks. It did help, and Thomas arrived early, as promised. He seemed a bit subdued, but simply said he thought, considering my condition, it would be best to take the horse and cart. Robbie was getting it rigged while I got my shawl and bonnet. Once we got in, I turned to him and asked him what he'd found out. He told me the price was pleasingly low as the family was in a hurry to settle the matter. "Yes. And?' I questioned him with my brows raised. "It's on Corke

Street past Chairman's Lane, so it is a bit of distance from your parent's, and more so because it's quite a steep climb. Which is why we're taking the cart."

I was taken a bit back. I wasn't very familiar with the homes in that area, but I told him it wasn't as though I was an old crone who couldn't climb a hill, or maybe we could keep the horse and cart since Da used it so seldom. He had his favorite horse, Blackguard, when he needed it and Mam had no desire to travel further than a walk to church and town. We both brightened up with the thought. I soon saw he was right though; it really was a steep hillside. We started watching anxiously for the house in question. The agent said he had put a blue cloth on the doorway and for us to take our leisure as the door was unlatched. There was quite an assortment of homes. All were small and made of stone, but some were rather forsaken looking and others as sweet and homey as one could wish. Those yards were filled with colorful flowers and neat paths. Suddenly we saw the blue cloth. Thomas stopped the cart, and we both sat there silently taking in the sight of this potential home of the Lydons. To say it had been neglected would be an understatement. The small front yard garden was so overgrown, you couldn't see what had been planted for what had decided to take root and choke it out. It was two stories, but quite narrow with only two windows downstairs, both covered with shutters, although one was barely hanging by leather straps. We turned to each other, waiting for one of us to speak first. Finally, Thomas murmured, "We've come this far, we may as well look inside. Nothing's wrong with the outside which some hard work won't put to rights." I felt this was a true statement, but overly optimistic.

Thomas came around and handed me down, took my arm and told me to be adventurous as he led me to the door. The stones in front of the doorway were all a-jumble so I stepped carefully around them as we entered together. The interior was dark, considering we had just come in from the sunlight and the shutters were closed (well, nearly closed!) I wasn't surprised to smell the underlying odor and sound of scurrying creatures. However, my nostrils were also assaulted by a very strong smell of decay. As our eyes adjusted to the dim light, Thomas went over and opened one of the shutters. As I suspected, there was no glazing in the windows; just the shutters. Once the light was allowed to enter, we could see the reason this house was selling at such a low rate. As many homes were in Kinsale, it was built into an alcove dug into the cliff, using the cliff as the back wall of the house. At some time over the decades since this house was built, one of the many deep underground springs which provide so many of us with water, had made its way through the wall. The back wall of the building was a curtain of green slime.

"Oh, sweet Jesus Thomas. We can't live here, especially with a child."

"The agent told me about this, but his description gave no warning as to the extent. He said the wall could be cleaned up, a trench dug to divert the water flow and a new wall built in front of the cliffside. But I doubt it would make the place habitable.'

I agreed and pointed out as small as the place was, putting in a new wall would lose almost a third of the existing room. "Using the horse and cart for transportation won't work either. There's no place to keep them!"

Dejected and disappointed, we walked out and started back down toward home. Thomas put a comforting arm around me and said, "Don't despair Darlin'. We'll keep looking and your parent's have made it clear they are in no hurry to see us gone. I just feel badly because I know you would like a place of your own, but there's no hurry and you'll be grateful for being home and the extra the help when the little one comes along. Aye?"

I smiled at this kind man and told him not to fret. I would continue to pray, and we would find the right place when it was meant to be. Mam did her very best to try to look upset for us when we told her about such a wreck of a house, but I could see she was pleased to have us home for a bit longer.

During the evening, while mam and I were doing some mending, she said, "Fi, I hope you don't mind, but I told the mid-wife Mrs. O'Brien we might drop by tomorrow morning. I know you're doing well, and I have no doubts all will go well. However, I cannot help but feel it would be best to have another woman, especially an experienced one to be here with us when the time comes. I am not as strong as I used to be, and I have usually been the one having the babe, not helping another who was giving birth. This will be my first grandchild and I would never forgive myself should something go awry because I didn't know what was needed. It pains me something fierce to admit this to you."

Reaching out and taking her hands I told her I would feel completely safe in her care. However, to relieve her of any fears and doubts, I would gladly go with her to Mrs. O'Brien's and see what she thought.

We arrived the next day about mid-morning and were welcomed with some refreshments. Inga O'Brien was a handsome woman who showed her Norse heritage. She came from a village far to the north of us in Scandinavia and, even after 25 years, she spoke with a strong accent. Her hair was thick and so fair it was hard to see the white hair overtaking the blond. She was a most respected mid-wife and I could see why. She was large without going to fat and strong, her hands large and capable. We spoke for bit and she invited us to call her Inga. After a short while, she said, "Vell, let's see vat ve haf here. Come here to my private room, yah?"

She led Mam and me into a little alcove with a curtained doorway. She had me remove my cloak and stand in front of her as she slowly walked around me. "Yah, a goot strong young voman Goot bones. Goot hips. I tink dis is a first, Yah?"

She felt down my back and put her hands on my protruding stomach. With a slight lifting motion, she nodded her head and said, "dis child will coming to see us soon I tink."

Mam exclaimed, "Oh yes, it should be about mid-August."

Inga's hands suddenly stopped moving. As I glanced at her, her ice blue eyes were looking intently into mine, her almost white eyebrows arched in a mute question. I felt my face blush as I could so plainly see she knew the child was going to arrive much sooner. I kept my eyes locked on hers with a silent plea she not give away my secret. A kindness flashed across her face and a slight smile on her lips reassured me she would not embarrass me.

"Hmmm? Dis seems to be a goot sized babe and I tink it will be coming more sooner den later. Is going to be an early bird, dis one."

I closed my eyes in relief and placed my hand over hers in a sign of gratitude. My mother just smiled and said she thought it was wonderful. We thanked Inga for seeing us and told her we would send for her when it looked like it was time. She gave us some instructions on how long to wait before contacting her for she had no desire to sit for hours for nothing if it was too soon! She also told me what I needed to have on hand and ready for her. Mam and I left for home feeling an excellent decision had been made and both of us felt less anxious.

July came in with a vengeance. The extra warmth we would have appreciated in January seemed to have held itself in reserve to show up now, increasing the temperatures of the usually warm, but mild, summer. Even the sea breezes turned contrary. Instead of blowing a cooling breeze, the moisture lay still and heavy over the harbour. The sun heated it until it felt as though one was standing over a steaming laundry cauldron. Bridget and Meg got up in the cooler wee hours to do the necessary baking, then we could expect meals which took little to no cooking for the rest of the day. I was miserable. I couldn't sleep and when I dozed, I would awaken covered in perspiration and sodden linens. Thomas, bless his heart, set up a cot in the room for himself for I couldn't bear his extra body heat in bed. Truth be told, it probably helped him sleep better too and since he had to go to work, sleeping well was important. I felt as large as a heifer, my breasts which filled out so pleasantly in the beginning now felt like two hot bags of pudding resting on my stomach. My ankles were swollen, my back ached, I was irritable with everyone. Even my patient Mam, loving Thomas and sweet Chloe were starting to avoid me and, on top of all of it, I was having to make way too many visits to the chamber-pot. I didn't care what the rumormongers said. This babe could not come too soon for my liking.

I woke up on July 20th, amazed I had slept so well, then I noticed the curtain at my window was moving and I felt cool air on my brow. Ah! The heat had broken. I lumbered out of bed noticing Thomas was already up and about. Washing myself at the basin, I looked forward to keeping a fresh feeling for the day instead of feeling sticky within the hour. I could sense the difference downstairs too. Everyone's spirits were lifted, and some neglected tasks were being tended to. I told Mam I would help with the dusting. She gave me a hug and told me to take it slow and easy as she had discovered dust was very good about waiting until one got to it!

About an hour later, I was reaching up to get the scrollwork on the cabinet and suddenly gasped as a sharp pain clutched at my abdomen. Sitting quickly, it slowly eased, and I told myself that apparently reaching up was not something my body wanted me to do. Over the next hour I felt a few twinges. Even though they were mild, I decided it would be best to go upstairs and rest a bit. I went into the kitchen to tell Mam I'd be upstairs, and she thought it was a good idea. I got about halfway up when I let out a cry as I doubled over in pain. Mam and Chloe ran quickly to the stairs, just as my water broke. I stood there staring at this puddle in dismay, thinking I had wet myself. Mam was at my side in moments, reminding me about the water breaking, and supported me as she got me to the bed. By this time Bridget, Meg, and Chloe were all there and Mam was giving orders like a general. She had

Chloe stack some flannels on the chair by the window, so I could sit there to get the cooler air. She had the girls make up the bed placing the linen over a sheet of canvas. Someone was sent to bring a pitcher of cool water from the well. I watched all of this in a rather detached manner wondering at the intensity and rushing about they were all doing until I was hit with another deep and undulating pain. It felt like the rolling of a ship only it was inside of me and it hurt! I was suddenly very afraid. I wanted to tell Mam I changed my mind. I didn't want a babe. She must have seen the fear in my eyes for she came to me, hugged me and held my hands as she consoled and reassured me.

"Fi, my darlin' girl. Don't fret. Women have been doing this since Eve and you are young and healthy with no reason to believe it will be overly difficult, nor should your babe be anything but healthy, even though it's coming a bit early."

Just then, another pain came, took a bit to peak and then subsided.

"But Mam, it hurts like the devil himself is in there!"

"I know, I know, dear one. Just try to ride each one out. Every pain means you're a step closer to you holding your own sweet child."

She was wise to not tell me the discomfort I was feeling now was but a shadow of what would come later. Sometimes it is best to be ignorant.

The girls got me settled into bed with several large pillows behind me. Chloe quietly came up to our mother and asked if I would be alright. Mam saw her distress and now took time to comfort her. I'm sure the recent passing of wee Kate made Chloe much more aware of the dangers we face in this world.

"Giving birth is a bit of a messy and noisy affair Chloe, but necessary. I guess it's our way of letting the world know we will fight, scream and battle to keep God supplied with children who will love and honor Him. One of the miracles is once the child is born, we quickly forget the pain and suffering and bask in the joy."

I called my little sister over to the bed and told her how wonderful it would be for our new babe to have such a marvelous, beautiful and charming Auntie Chloe.! Her face lit up like a sunrise. Suddenly, her little face showed concern and she asked Mam if someone shouldn't go get Thomas and the mid-wife.

"No darlin'. First babes have a habit of taking their time in arriving and Thomas would be of no use to any of us, pacing around and fretting. Also, Mrs. O'Brien had made it clear she has no desire to sit around waiting for events to finally get to the final stage."

Mam's birthing stool had already been brought out from storage and had been cleaned up for this occasion and was placed by the bed now. Mam suggested I walk around a bit for it would bring the babe sooner. I did so but would periodically be gripped by a fierce pain. Doubled over, Mam and Meg, or Bridget would support me until the pain let up and I could walk again. This went on for hours and I would rest in bed for a little while before walking again. Suddenly, the sharp twinges became more intense and were coming closer together. My mother immediately sent for Inga and Thomas, stressing to Bridget that Mrs. O'Brien was the priority. Time slowly lost all meaning. I was simply existing between gasping agony and waiting for the next wave. I was eventually aware of Inga's presence and was hopeful this meant it would soon be over. She had me lie down and examined me. I was vaguely aware this should be embarrassing but I was well past caring. She gave me a few sips of most appreciated water and told Meg to make sure there was hot water and a warmed clean blanket ready for when the babe came as both of us would need a some cleaning up. Through the agony I was aware of her presence being reassuring, and I could also see it in my mother's face. Mam held my hands and murmured dear things to me.

I was groaning quite loudly now and suddenly the door opened. Thomas burst in; his eyes wide and his face white with fear.

Mam quickly said, "She's fine, she's doing just fine. Come give her a kiss on the forehead and go away. She doesn't need you fussing about and you don't need to see such private things. Go back downstairs and accept you will hear quite a ruckus up here. The screaming helps the mother force the child out into the world. I would also recommend you and her Da, when he gets here, have several drinks. Now be gone!"

He kissed me, with tears in his eyes, and knowing better than to argue with Mam, departed as requested. Within thirty minutes, Inga had me on the stool and placed Mam and Meg behind me to wipe the sweat from my brow, support me and to massage my lower back. I made good use of the handholds as I strained to push. I sensed Inga's excitement as she let me know the babe's head was visible. Four more shriek inducing pushes and I felt the babe slip out of me and into Inga's large strong hands. I nearly collapsed with relief when I heard a wavering, high pitched cry.

"Is a girl!" Inga declared, "Is fine healthy girl. Vere is dat blanket and vater? Come, come Fiona. I make her cleaned for you. You hold your new dotter. Yah?"

I held out my hands to finally accept this little red-faced bundle. Holding her to my breast I cried tears of relief and joy. I wasn't the only one. Mam, Meg and Bridget were too. Chloe was just standing there with a huge grin and a look of amazement on her face. With a grunt, I looked at Inga in surprise as I felt another contraction. She smiled and said not to worry, it was the afterbirth and it would appear quickly with little discomfort. She was right. She efficiently went about cleaning up as the babe and I were taken to the bed. Once all was in order and Inga checked the babe once more, she went downstairs and advised the new father his wife and beautiful daughter awaited him. He took the stairs two at a time and had such a look of wonder on his face it couldn't help but touch me to the bottom of my heart.

"Josephine Kathleen Lydon, I would like to present you to your Father. But you may call him Da!"

Kneeling quickly by the bedside, Thomas brushed my dampened hair away from my forehead and asked if I was alright. I assured him I was.

"I have to say I was more than a bit frightened my love. I don't believe I've ever heard such blood-curdling screams before, and all for this wee little package. He softly pulled back the corner of the blanket and got a good look at his daughter. Yes, I told myself, she was his daughter no matter what!

"She's a might red and wrinkled. Is she supposed to look that way?"

Laughing, I told him she'd spent months floating about inside me and had just had a rough journey to greet us, so yes, all was well. I promised him she would improve greatly. Smiling with relief, he ran his fingers gently over her tiny head with its soft cap of downy blue-black hair. I knew I had made the right decision then, in more ways than one.

"Ah! Look," he exclaimed, "her eyes are blue like yours."

Mam smiled and informed him, "All babes start with blue eyes Thomas. It may be many months before we know if they will darken."

Thomas took Josephine's tiny hand between his thumb and first finger, marveling at this miniature appendage when she suddenly clenched her fist around his finger.

"Look! Look at her. Not even an hour old and so strong. I think she knows I'm her Da."

One glance at his face and I knew he was smitten, and God had blessed Josephine with just the right man to be her father.

She was soon fussing and rutting about. It was time to introduce her to what would become her major focus for months to come. Inga chased Thomas out of the bedroom and showed me how to help Josephine find the nourishment she sought. It seemed hopeless for a bit and I'm not sure which one of us was more frustrated, but she was certainly more vocal about it. Suddenly it all came together, and she latched on with a surprisingly painful fury. Once attached, there was no going back, and we all let out a sigh of relief. My journey into motherhood was obviously accomplished as Inga went about packing up her supplies, gave me a kiss on the forehead and said her farewells to all. Meg brought me some bread, soup and ale which I devoured. According to Bridget who had been downstairs, the new father and grandfather were well on their way celebrating their new status. Mam said she would be sure to have Thomas tucked away safely with Robbie and Colum so as not to disturb me or the babe. Within a very short time after Josephine's little mouth grew slack at my breast, I slipped into an exhausted, but peaceful sleep.

Our lives picked up a new meaning as each day was more special with a babe in the house. Her baptism was a relief to me as I felt this rite purified any sin which might have been carried over from the conception and the secret I kept from Thomas.

No evening meal was complete without at least one reference to something Josephine did. Thomas left the house in the morning as late as possible, so he would have more time with his daughter, and then would hurry home in the evening. I would spend the lovely days of summer in the garden with her. She slept well, but when she was awake, she missed nothing. The bright dapples of sunlight caught her eye. The colors of flowers, the movement of the leaves, the flitting birds and butterflies made her coo. At first, her fat little arms would flail about aimlessly as she tried to touch something, but before we knew it, we could see she was trying desperately to get her coordination to catch up with her quick eyes. We would soon have to be more cautious about what might be within her reach! She cooed and grunted in an obvious attempt to talk to us. By this time, the family had shortened her name to Josie which fit her bubbly exuberance more than the formal sound of Josephine. Thomas was beside himself with joy when he came home from work one day and Josie's arms and legs waved and kicked in obvious excitement showing she not only recognized him but was as excited as if he was Father Christmas.

We were still not having any luck finding a home, As the months wore on, Kinsale's port became as busy, if not busier, than it was before the battles. Housing was now at a premium, assuming one could even find one to buy, or lease. My parents stressed they were in no hurry for us to leave, but I could see Thomas was more than ready to be master of his own house. One early September evening, he told us all he had been checking on some land for sale and had a couple of spots picked out. He said they were both of a decent size for a yard, garden and a place for one, or two sheep.

"I've saved enough, thanks to your generosity Francis, to pay for one of them outright. The one I'm hoping for is a reasonable walk to here and has a lovely view of the harbour and river. By January we should be able to hire a stonemason to start the building. It will be small to start, but I will be sure it's designed to be enlarged as our family grows." He smiled at me with a gleam in his eye! "What do you think of such a plan Fiona?"

"Oh my! What a clever solution. How long do think it would be before we could move in?"

"I can't say for sure, but the winter rains shouldn't slow down the stonework, unless it's excessively cold and wet, but the finishing and roof may be delayed by the weather. If all goes well, and you don't mind very little furniture to start, I would think we might move in about May, or June."

I hugged him with tears in my eyes and told him I thought it was just splendid. Mam and Da said they would miss us being around, but they knew and understood how important this was to us. We all raised a glass to this new plan.

By December Josie learned to rollover and do all those delightful things we parents rave about to others. She was, however, showing a strong will and let us know how frustrated she was when she couldn't make her wee body do what she wanted it too. She could roll over from her stomach to her back, but not from her back to her stomach. This was fine for a bit, but she would soon howl so I spent a fair amount of time turning her back on her stomach, only to have her squeal in delight when she ended up on her back again. Mam reassured me she would learn to do both within a month, and I could count on her finding a new challenge for me to fuss about.

The weather turned crisp and colder, but we had many days without rain and Thomas found Alfred, a stonemason for our new home. We all spent quite a few evenings going over plans for the house and Alfred said he didn't see why he couldn't get started now, while the weather was fair. Doing this, he explained, he could have a good start before the Christmas Festivities kept all occupied.

One morning I found Mam crying softly in the sewing room. I knelt in front of her and placing my hands upon her knees, I asked her what was wrong. Was she ill?

"No, no, my dear Fi. It's just I miss my little Katy so sorely. I was sure she would be my last but was also sure she would be here to comfort me in my old age, and I would leave this earth well before her. This season has brought it all back for she dearly loved Christmas and this is when she and I would go afield in search of greens and red berries. We would share a cup of hot cider while I helped her with her needle work for gifts. I would tell her stories. Her favorites were the ones which mixed up a combination of faeries and Christ's birth. It mattered not to her."

Pressing her apron to her face, she started to sob again. I stood and held her close.

"Oh, my dearest mother. I am so sorry for your pain. I know we have all been touched by her absence, but I know the ache must be doubly deep for you. I truly wish I could make it easier for you. I wish I could take away your grieving."

"Oh Darlin', the grieving never goes away. It just becomes more bearable. I couldn't lose the grieving without losing the memories, so I don't want that. I must remember how blessed I am to have you home and wee Josie to help fill the hole in my heart. Don't fret should any of us cry for God gives us the tears to soothe the pain."

THE NEW YEAR 1603 - KINSALE

Our Holidays were blessed, and the house filled with laughter and hope as we greeted a new year. When the weather was fine Thomas would take us up to the lot to check on the progress of the stonework. Da visited too and declared it a grand piece of property.

Josie was sitting up now and trying desperately to communicate. Nothing was lovelier than to hear her squeals of delight when her ever increasing number of cousins played with her. Her beautiful black hair was turning wavy and thick. It shone like a black gem and her eyes had darkened to a deep blue with enchanting green flecks. I tried desperately to ensure she wasn't spoiled terribly. The only thing which saved her from being so was a personality which soaked up the love and attention as though it was the elixir of life. The most difficult thing was getting her down to sleep. It was as though she couldn't spare a moment away from learning and explorations. The world fascinated her and those in it adored her dimpled smile and good nature. We finally discovered her father's voice when reading to her eased her restless spirit. Her bright eyes would quietly watch his face intently whether he was reading a classic in

Latin, or a children's tale of witches and ghosts. Within minutes, she would be sound asleep, garnering her energy for a new day.

These months were like a honeymoon for us. The security we had at home and the help I had in caring for Josie, allowed Thomas and me to grow closer; to learn more about each other as man and woman and to respect each other's individuality. Thomas spent much time in not only telling me about his days and plans, but openly asked for my thoughts and opinions. I knew many women whose husbands wouldn't think of asking such of their wives, let alone value their input. When I prayed now, I didn't lament about the unfairness, or cruelty of the Spaniard's attack. Instead I offered up prayers of thanksgiving for having this beautiful precious child and a husband who made me want to please him in all ways. This was not the love portrayed in the current books and plays, of knights and fair damsels living in fairytale castles. This was a love grown with much sturdier roots to support a tree which would live for a lifetime. My life was truly a gift from God.

Early one evening in late February, there was a rap at the door. Mam and Da looked up. surprised at this unexpected event, as Bridget answered the door.

Her mouth dropped open as she exclaimed, "Paddy! What are you about?'

There in the doorway with his face turning red, stood one of the dock men wearing rough attire, a wool scarf and gloves which were more holes than yarn.

"Good e'en to ya Bridgit. It's glad I am to be seein' ya, but I'm here to deliver a message to Master Thomas, if he be home."

Hearing this father said, "Well Bridgit, bring the lad in out of the cold. Thomas is right here Paddy."

In he shuffled taking his large floppy hat off and holding it tightly to his chest. Thomas arose and asked what he had for him.

"Well sir this letter came off one of the ships arriving today but didn't get to the office until you had been well gone. I was told it said it was to be given to ya immediately and seein' as how I knew where ya were, I volunteered to bring it right away."

Thomas suspected his willingness might have had more to do with Bridgit's employment here than Paddy's desire to see Thomas.

Paddy stood a wee straighter as he formally took two steps forward and delivered packet into Thomas's hand.

"Well, thank you Paddy," said Thomas "what a kind thing to do on a bitter night."

Handing Paddy a coin, he said, "Here's a bit of gratitude to stand you to a drink at the public house where a warm fire will be a comfort. Bridget, take Paddy to the kitchen and see to it he gets a bowl of the wonderful dish we had tonight. I suspect you'll both enjoy the company."

After the two of them headed toward the kitchen, we all sat forward as Thomas opened the letter and held it to the light and read it aloud.

 *The Honourable East
India Company
Philpot Lane, London
Under Royal Charter of
Her Majesty Queen Eliz.*

*Mssr. Thomas Lydon
Gearaghty Import-Export
Kinsale Ireland
    February 15, 1603*

*Dear Sir: While in search of men of
reliable stature and abilities, we have
been apprised by numerous
references, including Lord Lynch of
Galway, in Ireland indicating you may
be of benefit to our company. Our
trade throughout Europe, and new
routes to the Mediterranean and India
has been expanding. We are seeking
an experienced man in the shipping
trades with extensive language skills to
manage the Portsmouth office and
handle the correspondence and
meticulous records required in our*

concern. This post would entail periodic travel to our London office and possibly travel to some of our foreign ports.

We would like to discuss this in more detail to determine if our association with you would be mutually beneficial, preferring to have this meeting happen no later than the end of March in this year in order to take advantage of our slower period and to have time to train you in our methods before the seas are more accommodating to heavy traffic.

It is our understanding you have a family and even though this position comes with a household in Plymouth, should you be engaged, we ask your family not join you for the first three months of your tenure to ensure your focus will be upon your duties.

Enclosed you will find a list of ships and sailing schedules out of Corke, Ireland. You may book passage on any *available vessel, using the pass included. Please advise us of your plans and we will arrange transportation to our London office upon your arrival. Should you wish to decline this offer, be so kind as to let us know immediately so we may continue our search.*

Most respectfully,

Robert Fitzgibbons, Esq.

There was a sudden silence as we all looked at each other dumb founded. The fire in the grate continued to spit and hiss, there was the soft murmuring of conversation from the kitchen, but we were as mute as posts.

Clearing his throat, a couple of times Thomas finally said, "This is an amazing letter! It will take a fair amount of discussion as it will affect all of us. Of course, I am flattered to be considered by such a noted firm and to know Lord Lynch put my name forward with such good report. However, assuming I would get the posting, I owe you much loyalty Francis and would feel it inconsiderate at best to leave you short-handed. There's also the time I must be away from hearth and family. To not be with Fiona and Josie for such a stretch would pain me deeply, as I know it would pain all of you to have them eventually be placed so far away from Kinsale and all they love. Last, but not least, this is asking a lot of Fiona to not only move away, but to settle in England where the Irish are not thought well of and to give up on our current dreams here."

Father spoke up first, "Thomas, you are young and have much to offer. Of course, I have grown to depend on you. However, Robbie and Colum have learned much from you and it may well be time to let them handle more of the burdens. After all, this will become their business. A good man like you needs to grasp such opportunities when available, for such are few and far between. Should you agree to meet with them, there are two outcomes. One is, they see the value in you, and you feel the offer is fair and bodes well for your career. Two, you are not a good fit for them, or they for you, then you can come home and pick up where you left off."

I hadn't said anything yet, but Mam and I both had tears in our eyes. Thomas's eyes met mine and I could read the questions in them.

Taking a deep breath and with a bit of a quaver in my voice, I simply said, "I can see this would be a wonderful prospect dear, but such a huge change from what we planned. I cannot even imagine being separated from you for so long. Even as children you were always near. Then, well then having to live so far…" My voice caught in my throat and I could say no more.

Thomas stood, reached down and took my hand, "My love, tis nothing which must be decided this moment." Turning to Da, "If you wouldn't mind, I think Fi and I need to discuss this in our room as we both have many questions and concerns."

"Of course. Of course, as do Mary and me. We'll revisit this offer in the morning and bid you both a blessed night."

Entering our room, Thomas pulled me close and let me cry on his chest for a while until I raised my eyes to him and asked, "Is this something you are truly considering Thomas?"

"Yes. I really must try. Your father is so good to us and I would do anything for him, but I have been missing the challenges I had in Galway and I know your brothers are chafing at the bit to do more than they are allowed. I have noticed your brother Robbie mooning over the apothecary's daughter, Margaret, and he may soon have a desire to move up in the business! Oh, Fiona, I know this will be a hardship, but we'll only be apart for a short period of time. You are so busy with Josie; the time will fly by. Plus, your worry may be for naught as I may not be the man for the job, and I'll hurry home as quickly as possible."

"Oh," I exclaimed, "what about our house? It should be done by spring and we may be in England by then."

"Yes, yes, you're right." He sat down and furrowed his brow while pondering this. A smile appeared as he explained, "Unless they offer me considerably less than I earn now, I can continue to pay to have the cottage finished because the letter said the post comes with a household, which I would assume means it would be ours as long as I was employed. Once the cottage is complete, and assuming I will remain in their employ, we can increase our income by leasing it out, minus a small fee to the agent. When we do return to Kinsale, we will have our cottage waiting!"

I felt my heart lighten as I realized this would mean there would always be a home for me in Kinsale. We decided to sleep on it and see what additional questions might need to be addressed in the morning.

At breakfast it was obvious the whole family understood the sacrifices and the courage it would entail to undertake such a challenge. Yet, we all agreed it was worth the risk.

Thomas had passage booked for the third of March which, barring weather, would make landfall in Bristol on the fifth. When receiving confirmation of his travel documents, he was pleased to see he was assigned one of the cabins instead of steerage below decks. He felt this bode well for the company's desire to treat him well. He made sure he had sufficient funds to cover any expenses should the company not cover his passage home if he was not engaged. He always believed in hoping for the best and planning for the worst! I was not the only one with tears in my eyes as we all wished him God's protection upon his departure. Da left explicit instructions should any correspondence arrive for him, on any of his ships, that it was to be delivered to him post-haste at his office, or residence.

We got a letter from Thomas on the thirteenth.

March 9, 1603 - Dearest Family: I am safe here in London. I arrived in good time in Bristol after a somewhat sea tossed voyage. As short as the trip was, I was most pleased to set my feet upon solid ground. HEIC was as good as their word and I was met within the hour by a representative. He bought me a meal at the local public house and seemed intent on heaping laud and honor on the Company. I wasn't sure if this was a good sign or not. However, he was a most pleasant young man and truly did seem to take pride in his employment with them. He is assigned to the Bristol office, so he gave me a note of passage on the post stage to London and advised me where to wait at the depot in London for my escort. It is about 120 miles to London, so I planned on a journey of four or more days. I was pleasantly surprised. The Post Road system is a wonder. The roads are well kept, and fresh horses are in supply at each stop. By the time we bought refreshments and took care of our personal needs, the horses and drivers had been replaced and we were on our way. The weather held well, and I arrived early on the third day. I was taken to an inn and told I could freshen up there and was invited to attend a mid-day meal at the office. A coach would be waiting for me at 1:00 p.m. Upon my arrival, I was led to a private room where an impressive meal was laid out and we commenced to discuss the role of a manager in Portsmouth, and my qualifications, or lack thereof. They are gentlemen held in high-esteem and yet treated me with utmost courtesy. I felt they were most interested in my experience handling the business from afar in Galway and my language skills. I believe they thought speaking English would have been more engrained in Ireland than the Gaelic. However, as they expand to northern ports, they are finding more manifests and correspondence in the Irish, thereby needing a native speaker to translate. They are also expanding in the Mediterranean where there are many dialects. I feel the afternoon went well. This was all yesterday, and I have been instructed to wait for their decision, or further questions. They told me should they ask me to stay, they will then discuss wages and advantages and I can accept or decline. This is allowing me some time to explore and there is much to see. London is an amazingly large city. The streets and *the River Thames are excessively crowded, even unto the night! There are so many lanterns one wonders where they get the oil keep them all going. I have been to St Paul's Cathedral and the menagerie of animals at the Tower of London. I preferred the cathedral. If I get the posting, I will be most grateful we will be living in Portsmouth and not London. I hear Portsmouth is not nearly as large and is cleaner. I think we will both be more comfortable nearer the sea. I will write immediately when I know the way of it. I miss you all. Give sweet Josie a cuddle and a kiss from her Da.*

We were so pleased to hear from him and know that all was going well. Da pointed out he felt Thomas would be well received and we should be prepared for an offer being made.

"I knew that lad was destined for more than clerking for me! It is not like a company such as the Honourable East India to spend time and money to interview a candidate unless they were quite sure he would be worth the effort. I have little doubt Thomas made a most favorable impression. It now will depend on the compensation and if they follow through with any promises they have made. The arrangements to get him to London certainly shows a penchant for keeping their word."

Mam reached over and closed her hand over mine. I knew Da was probably right, but there wasn't much I could do until we knew and then we'd have several months before Josie and I would be allowed to travel to England to be with him. Just thinking of it made my stomach feel queer. There were a fair number of the English in Kinsale, and I had met many in Galway. It was rather like cats and dogs co-existing in the same household. I accepted them, but I didn't understand them and their feelings of superiority. Ireland had existed just fine with our Tribal and Clannish system long before they had their single monarchy and for many decades, people from England, Scotland and Europe came to Ireland for education. The English and Irish were different breeds and I would be moving into their kennel!

As expected, we had a letter from Thomas within the week and he was offered the post. I could sense his excitement at the prospect and his relief in being offered substantially more than Da could ever pay him. He said he had not seen our new home in Portsmouth, but it was described as, "Being for a man of good stature and would include a housekeeper and a cook, at the Company's expense."

We were shocked at such fortune. I could hardly believe it. Then Thomas went on to explain it was the company's way of ensuring my wife would be free to fulfill her duties, such as entertaining merchants and traders and ensuring our 'home' reflected the status and prosperity of the HEIC. My eyes went wide with fear.

"Oh, Mam! I shan't have an idea of how to be such a wife. I will be a great embarrassment to him."

She smiled reassuringly to me. "I think you are being too hard on yourself. You really do know much more than you think. You have helped me do the same thing for your father and his business associates. The only difference will be you'll be doing it in a grander house, with finer tableware and lovely gowns! Think upon Lady Lynch's house, her parties and her treatment of her guests and you'll have the perfect pattern to follow." Laughing, she said, "The real secret sweet Fiona is to have more than enough to eat and drink for all and to ask your guests questions which will allow them to brag about their lives, their wives and their exploits."

Thomas was right. The days were flying by and mother made sure to take me under her wing to a much greater degree in planning dinners and directing Bridgit and Molly. Chloe went through some sad times when thinking about not having sweet Josie around. They were so very close, and each was the delight of the other. About ten days later, Thomas sent some money so I might freshen my wardrobe in anticipation of my arrival. Of all things, he included a woman's publication with sketches of some of the newer styles in London! Mam and I laughed together over some of them as they were quite outlandish, but I found the more conservative ones to be more my style. I realized several of my better clothes could be easily updated with wider ruffs, cuffs, or collars. Colorful embroidery was also more in use. The hats and bonnets might have to be purchased after I got there. They were taller than our style here and quite dressed in feathers, ribbons and lace. The drawings also gave me insight into hairdressings. I noticed many of them leaned toward the curls the Queen had made fashionable, but there were others which I thought would be more flattering for me. After putting Josie down for the night, I would sit at my dressing table and play at styling my hair in such fashions. It wasn't too long before I mastered several which I thought would work for me.

Thomas also apologized for not writing as much as he would like, but said he was on the move from sunrise until late evening when his candle burned out. He had a tutor to teach him some of the languages of India and to improve on some of the Mediterranean. dialects. He said he missed us terribly and begged I include the little stories of the household and wee Josie. He said I might also want to dust off the book of French Lady Lynch had given me for most people there, even if they didn't speak French, used many French phrases. He said he would help me with the pronunciation when we were together again.

I did as he suggested and also contacted my old school friend, Rose, the mayor's daughter. She had been sent to live with a cousin in Rouen France for two years and was delighted to help me in my studies. She also helped me see this trip to England as an adventure and a wonderful opportunity for Josie. Our afternoon lessons flew by and I so enjoyed her company.

We got a surprisingly short letter from Thomas toward the end of March and soon discovered we were not the only ones to hear the news he gave us.

March 25, 1603, Dearest Family: I must be brief as I wish to get this on the next packet heading to Kinsale. Queen Elizabeth died in London on March 24th. I believe she was quite old, possibly in her late sixties and had been in declining health. London, and of course the rest of England is in turmoil even though King James the VI of Scotland has been made King. He will be King James 1, of England and will retain his Scottish title too. Scotland and England shall now be under one crown. One doesn't know what to think by hearing the talk in the streets. There are many lamenting the passing of "Dear Queen Bess" where others are hoping the new King will encourage a return to open Catholicism. James was born a Catholic, but embraced Protestantism later, so I don't think that's going to happen. I'm sure we will be in for much Pomp and Ceremony in the coming weeks. Even

though, being Irish, her death does not tug at my heart
strings, it is an historic event and I am glad to be in the
midst of it! Nevertheless, I am counting the days until I
have you both in my embrace. The head office is hinting
that I am doing so well, they may be putting me in charge
of my office sooner rather than later. I will write again
when time permits, and I will let you know. Most
lovingly, Your Thomas.

We were stunned. It seemed she had always been
'The Queen', and one couldn't imagine another monarch.
Even though she wasn't ours by choice, she was the only
one we had. Da immediately grabbed his cloak and
headed down to the Government House. He knew it
would be wild with rumors and conjecture and he wasn't
about to miss a word of it. Mam made him promise he
would tell us EVERYTHING!"

As important as the news was about the Queen's
passing and the new King, I was more interested in the
last part of his letter. Could it be possible we could be
with Thomas sometime in May? It wasn't until later I
realized being with him was now over-riding my dread of
leaving my family.

The budding trees and blossoming flowers of April
reflected the activity and hope in our household and in
my heart. Chloe was invaluable in taking care of Josie
and keeping her from being underfoot, although I realized
this would make it even harder for my kind and soft-
hearted sister to say goodbye to the wee one. One day I
asked Chloe to walk with me in the garden.

"I hope you know I appreciate all you are doing with
the extra work and helping to take care of Josie too."

"I don't mind a bit for you know I love caring for her. You and Mam are so busy. I can't believe how much you need to do." There was a pause, then Chloe looked up at me and I saw the tears shimmering on her lower lashes. Taking my hand, she asked, "Aren't you afraid? It's a long way from home."

With a lop-sided smile, I admitted, "Oh Dear one, I'm frightened nearly to death! It's not so bad during the day when there's so much to think of and do, but when I lay alone at night and try to sleep, my fears haunt me. What if something bad shall happen at sea? What if Josie should be ill? What if Thomas isn't there when I land. Then, I will also have to be 'the lady of the house' for the first time in my life. Chloe I am so afraid I will fail Thomas and make a fool of myself. Should such a thing happen, I can't run home. I will be stuck in a strange land with no friends or family."

By now my own tears had spilled over and we were hugging each other in our despair.

My little sister reassured me I would not fail Thomas, just because I was too stubborn to do so. That did get a smile out of me and as we walked, we tried to speak of it as an exciting escapade and to think of the things I would see and learn. She made me promise to write often and to be sure the letters were filled with details. I turned to her suddenly and said.

"Maybe you can come over for a visit! Wouldn't it be grand? Now I'm not promising because I don't know what benefits might come with Thomas's position and none of us could afford paying for your passage, but if it's at all possible, we must do it!"

Chloe's face was sunshine itself! The enthusiasm of youth took over and she embraced the idea within moments. Before we knew it, we were talking of the things we would do together, even the possibility of her getting to see London.

By the end of April, I had received a letter from Thomas with the appropriate documents for our voyage on May twelfth. It was especially good news as he was able to arrange it so we could leave from Kinsale and arrive directly to Portsmouth. This would save us the trip to Corke and the need to arrange any other transportation. Since Josie was so little and I would be traveling on my own, this was a great relief. For the next two weeks, it seemed we all kept finding opportunities for quick hugs, the touching of hands and quiet evenings talking of memories we all shared. I packed and repacked and Mam was determined to put enough food in my hamper to feed the entire crew. I asked Da hundreds of questions about traveling by sea. I had been on many boats, but never large vessels and I had never been on the open sea. He said he knew the Captain well and would ask him to take steps to ensure I was treated well and had any help I might need on the trip. His reassurance kept my nervousness under some bit of control.

MAY 1603 – AT SEA

May twelfth arrived, and we were all up early. Fortunately, Josie slept well, but I doubted I had dozed for more than an hour. My mind was wild with questions to which I had no answers and fears over which I had no control. Da reassured me the weather between Kinsale and England was being reported as fair and if Josie and I stayed bundled up while on deck, we should be quite comfortable.

The whole family came on board to see me off and to help me get settled in our little cabin. Josie's eyes were darting everywhere at all the new sights, sounds and smells. My family stayed until it was clear the ship, the Tawney Rose, was preparing to depart. Tears were streaming down my face, as it was Mam's and Chloe's. Even Da's eyes glistened. Of course, Colum and Robbie were more interested in the activity on deck and how the seamen worked the rigging and all with such skill. However even they gave Josie and me warm hugs and kisses before going ashore. We looked and waved to each other until they were out of sight. I took a deep breath and turned to look toward the bow as I now had to consider more where we were going, rather than where we had been. I took Josie into our cabin to change her clout and feed her. When we came out on deck again my mouth gaped. The headlands into Kinsale harbour were barely visible and the vastness of ocean ahead of us was beyond comprehension. Seeing the sea from the shore didn't capture the feeling of being surrounded by it. We were still close enough to see the gulls swirling and dipping into the whitecaps and the water was the deepest blue I had ever seen.

The next day, the Captain invited me to take our mid-day meal in his quarters with his officers. It was quite lovely and hard to believe, amongst the silver and china, that we were at sea. However, I did enjoy noting how tables, desks and chairs were built in such a way to prevent items from sliding about as the ship pitched in the ever-changing ocean. Very clever!

"I hope my ignorance is not too obvious, but I would like to ask you something Captain. I noticed by the sun we seem to be traveling south instead of east. Are we stopping at some other port before going to England?

A couple of his officers started to smirk, but one quick look from the captain erased any hint of the same and they were suddenly all very interested in their plates.

"First, let me say I am impressed you noticed and came to the correct conclusion. We are heading in a southerly direction. However, the answer is yes and no. We are heading south, but we are going to England straight away. You see England's southernmost tip is quite a bit south of Ireland's. If we were heading to Bristol, or Swansea, we would be on an eastern heading, but to get to Portsmouth, we need to go south and around Land's End before heading east and north east. Let me show you." He gallantly escorted me over to a table covered in a huge stack of maps bound together like a book. Pointing out locations on the map which showed our route, I could plainly see exactly what he was talking about.

"Amazing captain! My father has some books with maps in them and I have always been quite fascinated. However, his were much smaller and not nearly so detailed or beautifully drawn. Thank you for explaining."

The next day was fine with fair winds and scudding white clouds. I played with Josie on deck and I noticed quite a few of the crew would stop by and smile and coo at her. I'm sure many of them had children of their own at home and must miss them terribly when they sailed. After I put Josie down for a nap, I found a comfortable corner on deck and spent the early afternoon studying more of my French. However, by late afternoon I was sensing the sea was getting a little rougher and the temperature was dropping. I had no problem convincing myself to go back to my cabin and snuggle down there. By evening the rocking of the ship was making me feel the light supper I had wasn't quite light enough. I was certainly aware of mal de mer but had never experienced it. All I could hope now was my stomach would not rebel any more than it already was. I looked over at Josie as she played in her little makeshift bed and she didn't seem to be troubled at all. Thank the Lord for small blessings! I remembered the bits of bread which helped me with my nausea during my pregnancy, so I nibbled on a little hardtack before I lay down and it must have worked, for I drifted off to sleep without further upset.

Time went surprisingly quickly and then one evening the Captain mentioned we would arrive in Portsmouth the next day. My heart leapt at the thought of finally seeing Thomas again. I forced myself to think only of this longed-for reunion. The future would just have to be handled as it came.

As we entered the harbour about mid-day, I could see it was well fortified, but much more so than Kinsale. There were forts, towers and walls. One of the sailors mentioned Portsmouth was used by the Royal Navy. I was amazed at the multitude of boats, ships, buildings and people. Of course, now with winter storms at bay, almost anything which could float was either bringing things to sell or taking things elsewhere to be sold. The air was heavy with the familiar smells of tar, hides, fish and the brackish, briny odor of the harbour. Taking in the view of the harbour, I noticed it spread out in several directions with many docks and piers, all around. However, the most obvious difference to me was the lack of hills and cliffs. The landscape all around was almost completely flat and the town stretched for miles, where Kinsale was compact and its homes were stacked snuggly against ever increasingly higher hillsides.

I tried to look around for Thomas, but there were so many wharves, piers and warehouses, I had no idea where we would drop anchor. As we got closer to what was now clearly our anchorage, I started to fear Thomas wasn't there yet. Then, I spotted him. My eyes had already passed by him several times without recognition for he certainly looked different. His head, tilted down and to the right, to hear what the gentleman next to him was saying, was half covered by a flat green cloth cap. The jaunty white feather attached to it shone bright in the sunlight. He was wearing a calf length russet tunic belted around his slim waist and a cap- sleeved vest. His white shirt had full sleeves and sported a wide collar with long points in front laying over the neck of the vest. Even his soft fawn leather boots with the tops turned down was a new look for him. At this moment he turned his head up toward the sunlight and my heart filled with joy at the sight of his handsome face. He gave every appearance of a prosperous, successful, merchant and I felt a slight clutch at my heart as my fears of failure again came to the fore. As he continued to scan the decks for us, I pointed him out to Josie.

"Look darlin'! There's your Da. Isn't he such the gallant gentleman? "

At last our eyes met and one look at his smile reassured me we were as welcome a sight to him is he was to us.

It seemed to take forever to get everything ready for us to disembark, but I was eventually in his arms. Josie peeked out from under her bonnet but clung very tightly to me. Poor thing didn't remember him what with the time we were apart and the upheaval of the journey. Keeping his arm around my shoulders, Thomas started issuing orders to several men who were obviously there to assist him.   Thomas was full of questions while we waited. I had to reassure him Josie and I were both well. I told him wee Josie never seemed to suffer a moment from sea sickness, even when the water was rough. He smiled grandly and stated she obviously had the makings of sailor. I immediately had to erase the image of the Spaniard from my mind and changed the subject. In very short order, the men announced all was loaded and we rode with Thomas while the men followed us. Pointing to the south-east, Thomas said he could hardly wait to take me to see Southsea Castle.

"It was from this very castle old King Henry watched his favorite ship, the Mary Rose, sink during a battle with the French. She was huge! She could carry over 300 men. She sank in the waters between here and the Isle of Wight and it's so deep she couldn't be salvaged. However, the view from castle is splendid and a perfect spot to spend an afternoon."

I scooted closer to him and told him it was a wonderful idea. I smiled as I recalled our basket-lunch on Salt Hill in Galway. I suspected we wouldn't have as much privacy here. We turned onto High Street and left the dockyards as we entered a busy and well-appointed shopping district. The streets were laid out quite geometrically and broad, not meandering and narrow like at home. A couple of turns later we were on a street with an assortment of neat cottages, and larger manor houses with larger yards and longer drives to the houses themselves. I noticed one up ahead which was a bright white limestone with black window sashes and dark green hedges. I thought it was a very pleasant combination. I was even more surprised when Thomas turned into the driveway.

My mouth fell open when he said, "Welcome home Milady."

My imagination of where we would live varied from a most humble cottage, to a bit fancier version of the same, but never to such a lovely and large home. And to think it was ours, as long as Thomas was employed.

As Thomas escorted me up the steps, three people waited there to greet us.

"Fiona, this is Annie your housekeeper, this is Phoebe your kitchen maid and this is Peter, groundskeeper and also in charge of our carriage and horses."

The ladies curtsied and Peter bowed. I felt my face turn red at such signs of respect. I tipped my head at each and told Annie and Phoebe I looked forward to speaking with them after the babe and I got settled. Annie, tall and thin, asked me what time we would like to dine, but her accent was such broad Scots I had to ask her to repeat it. I looked at Thomas with raised brows and he told her about 8:00 would do fine.

We entered a foyer with a table in the center of the room filled with lovely flowers. The floor was made of stone, but a large portion of it was covered in an intricately woven carpet. There was a stairway to the right and an open double door into, what appeared to be a parlor. Thomas gave some instruction to Annie and he took Josie and me on a tour of the downstairs. The kitchen was bright, airy and clean. The back door opened onto a kitchen garden at least three times as large as ours at home. It was well cared for and was showing early signs of becoming very lush. The warm sunshine was already causing the herbs to release lovely scents into the air. Right off the kitchen was another set of double doors opening on to a dining room with several sideboards in dark wood and a fireplace at the far end of the room.

Noticing the painting hanging above the mantle I asked, "Who's the old gentleman with the fierce mustaches in the picture?"

"I'm afraid my employers assumed we and our guests would be honored to have the likeness of one of the founders keeping an eye on us while dining. I considered making up a story about him being some powerful and successful member of my family, but it would be just my luck to have someone know who he really was!"

Josie had been sleeping in my arms, but started fussing as it had been quite a while since she had been fed. "Oh Fiona, I'm sorry. I quite forgot about her. I'm afraid my fathering skills have fallen by the wayside. She obviously is hungry, and you must be exhausted. Let me take you up to our rooms so you'll have some privacy. I'll have Annie bring up something to eat and drink too."

As soon as he said it, I realized he was right. I could have sat down right there and gone to sleep.
were large and lovely. The bed was a four-poster draped in rose-colored cloth with a matching coverlet. It looked soft and inviting. There were two windows facing the southeast and from this room we could see the harbour. Although physically different, the scene was just enough like Kinsale to bring tears to my eyes. However, Josie's demands were getting quite vocal and quickly brought me back to the here and now. As I was getting settled in a chair to feed Josie, there was a light tap on the door.

"Come in." said Thomas and there was Annie with the promised tray of food. As she started to set it up on the table next to me, Thomas kissed my forehead, headed out the door and said he would see me after the babe, and I had a rest.

"There ye be milady. I dinna ken yer favorites, but thought a cup of broth, some bread and fruit would be to yer likin"

Catching most of what she said, I reassured her it looked just right and was most appreciated.

"Ah weel then, I'll be up in a jig to pour you some hot water for yer basin so's ye can freshen up. Then, if ye don't mind, I'll put the bairn down for a nap so ye may take a rest too. There's a wee bed for her next to yours, so you'll not have any worries as to her closeness."

"That sounds wonderful Annie. I can barely keep my eyes open."

A wide smile split her thin face and she was as good as her word. Once I washed up and my head hit the pillow, I slept for nearly two hours.

The next few weeks were spent putting my new home in order and adding to my husband's rather spartan idea of décor. Energetic little Annie was a Godsend. I was amazed at how much she could get done in a day, especially considering she had taken on extra duties with a child in the house. It was obvious Thomas was a happy man to have his wife and child with him again at last. He loved coming home and spending time with Josie on his knee while he sang, or read, to her. He and I often laughed at her serious expression when he read. She actually looked like she understood him! His attentions to me in the privacy of our rooms certainly let me know he had missed me too.

One evening while we spent some quiet time in front of the hearth, He mentioned we would need to have a supper party soon to introduce his family to his colleagues and their wives.

"Even though Portsmouth is larger than Kinsale, it's still has tightly knit groups, especially amongst the merchants and politicians. Believe me, much of what is accomplished on the docks is affected by the favors curried with the local government. My job is to keep a sharp eye on the administration and organization of our shipping, but it's also dependent on socializing and chatting with those in power. The good news for you is I have already done some entertaining before you came, so they are familiar with me and with each other. Once they arrive and are served food and drink, the conversations will flow quite readily. I have been getting some heavy-handed hints that the wives of my associates are most curious to meet you."

"I won't lie. I am nervous to meet these English ladies, although it's good they have already socialized with you. I do so want to make you proud. However, I'm not sure I will know what to say, or ask the men. I mean, after all my father was in the business, as are you, but I don't think I know enough to really voice an opinion or open a subject."

Thomas chuckled. "There's no problem at all. First, I don't think these men would even consider a woman would have an opinion about such matters. Their wives are more interested in the latest fashion and gossip! Plus, it's the easiest thing ever to start a conversation with the gentlemen. Simply ask them what they do, or where they're from, then sit back and listen. Most of them, but especially the politicians, exist fully believing the rest of the world is simply waiting for them to enlighten all with their rambling discourses on any variety of subjects."

His comments made me smile and did make me feel more confident.

"Well then, on another subject Thomas, I fear we will need to spend a fair amount for flowers, food and wine and I'm not sure I have anything appropriate to wear to such a gathering."

Thomas leaned forward and taking my hand explained. "Well, my love, I'm glad you brought this up as I have wanted to explain our situation to you. East India compensates me very well and we have a generous allotment for entertaining. I reassured my employers my wife was efficient and frugal. However, because you are, and more, I don't want you to skimp for it is expected we put on a proper event. Even though many of our guests could buy and sell me without a blink, they just adore eating and drinking from someone else's larder!" I will have Henry send you a list of attendees and of the provisioners we use. They will sell you just what you will need and put it on our account. "

"Henry?"

"Oh yes! You haven't met him yet. Henry Bell is my personal assistant. As bright, honest and hardworking a young man as you'd be likely to meet. I can't tell you how many hours this lad saves me! Henry will be at our supper too. Hmmm? He's not married, so I doubt he'd know anything about dressmakers. I'll have him ask around. He's met most of the merchant's wives, so he'd be a good judge as any as to their tastes in fashion. Being a bachelor, he's probably made special note of the looks of the women here about. I'll be sure he gets back to you as quickly as possible."

The time flew by in making preparations. I got the invitations out, discussed the menu with Phoebe and had found a dressmaker. A Madam Pinkerton who seemed to magically know what color and style would do, although I had to tone her down for I thought her original selection too flamboyant and above my station. Her seamstresses had fingers which practically flew, and I was reassured the gown would be ready well before the party. While at a fitting, madam held a lovely necklace with a single pearl which nestled perfectly at my bosom and had matching earbobs. I declined and explained it was not something I felt I should buy.

"Oh, my dear. There is no problem. We can use what I refer to a 'short term arrangement'. Many of my patrons use it. I loan them to you for the evening, you then only need pay a small fee for the loan and return them to me! Isn't that clever? What's even better, only a few of those on your guest list happen to use this service and most of them prefer something gaudier rather than the elegance of such a set. I doubt they will have any idea these are not yours. You will assuredly give these lovely pearls just the canvas they need for proper display."

The day of the party arrived, and the house was in such a bustle I hardly had time to be anxious. Annie helped me dress and was most reassuring.

"Aye! You look beyond bonny Miz Fiona! The fullness of yer skirts makes yer waist look as wee as a bird's and wearing your hair up shows off yer fair complexion and the pearls."

Thomas introduced me as the guests arrived and I did my best to fix the faces with the names. Henry Bell was easy. We hadn't met but had corresponded and he was a most pleasant and sincere young man. I was surprised he was still a bachelor for he was quite handsome and charming. I supposed it was due to his youth and the conservative nature of his clothing. It was of quality but got rather lost in the 'plumage' worn by the other cocks-o-the walk arriving. There was Lord Alfred and Lady Pembroke; such opposites! He was so heavy he waddled, and she was as thin as a stick. She was also wearing enough jewelry to open a shop. I was able to recall their name by assuming the Lady's penchant for gems kept them 'broke'. I met the Radcliffs who apparently were from somewhere in northwestern England and their accent was as thick as porridge. I simply nodded and smiled when conversing for I hardly understood a word. I was then introduced to Stanley Haverstead, Thomas's Assistant Manager. He was courteous enough, but the tall, bony man had a simpering quality which made it obvious he thought himself quite superior. His quiet little wife, Sarah, was more an appendage than a spouse. She was certainly dressed well enough, but the style and colors fit her not at all. Thomas had already explained to me the man's position as Assistant Manager was directly related to his uncle being on the HEIC's Board and little to do with his abilities or efforts. I then met the Strattons. Manfred Stratton was elderly and obviously not in the best health but with kind, sharp and inquisitive eyes. His welcome to me was warm and sincere. Then I met his wife, Eugenia. who was as much as twenty years younger than her husband. I was delighted to hear the lilt of my homeland in her voice. Small and quick with wavy dark hair, I couldn't help but think of a little chickadee.

She smiled and her face lit up as she was introduced. "It's grand to meet you at last. I was so pleased to hear you are Irish. One does get tired of hearing everyone talking through their noses and clipping their words as though they had scissors in their mouths."

I liked her immediately.

"It is certainly my pleasure Eugenia. Where is your family home and how long have you been here?"

"Please call me Gennie, all my friends do, Fiona. My family is from County Mayo, but I left to marry Manfred ten years ago. I used to go home occasionally, but his health makes me want to stay close by these days."

I asked her to call me Fi and she frequently made sure she was at my side, whispering asides to me of tidbits of information on my guests. One I found of interest was the reticent Mrs. Haverstead who seldom found her voice when in her husband's company. However, it seems her role was to be his champion when with the other wives. She spent much time bemoaning the fact her husband wasn't given the post of manager. It bothered her not one whit that I was the wife of the man filling this position. More than likely parroting Stanley's complaints, she went on about Thomas's 'ignorant' ideas, such as giving in too much to employee's requests, unnecessarily complex record keeping which created more work for poor Stanley and Thomas's efforts to compete with the Portuguese for the spices and silks of the East Indies.

Gennie, smiling behind her fan, told me. "If Haverstead worked half as much time as he spent sniveling about his position, he might actually achieve something.

The rest of the evening went well. However, even though I was received with appreciative attention from the men, Thomas was right. As soon as I interjected an opinion or asked for additional explanations on any subject the men were discussing, I was verbally patted on the head and ignored. I finally retired to the seating area where the ladies were gathered and got an earful of the less than exciting subjects of which they were concerned. I also noticed a pattern in their conversations. Even though there was much gossip, some of which might be wise for me know, something interesting happened when a woman would leave the group. The talk would immediately take a different direction and speculation would focus on the latest tales regarding the missing person. It's not that we didn't have our share of chin-wagging in Kinsale, it just seemed to verge more on the malicious in this group. Of course, fashions were discussed, planned purchases and expansions on homes, voyages, and the accomplishments of spouses and offspring. Many of the women politely congratulated me on my husband's posting, but the comments frequently carried an undercurrent of assuming it was luck rather than experience and skill. I tried to impress upon them how efficiently he handled such work in Kinsale and Galway.

"Oh my, undoubtedly," Lady Pembroke said, "But, after all it was in Ireland and isn't Kinsale (she pronounced it Kine-SELL) just a fishing village?"

"Hardly!" I responded and simply took a sip of wine to hide my blush and my irritation.

Thomas was well pleased with the event and received many compliments from his colleagues and friends. They felt I was charming and quite sharp witted, which was a rare compliment! He also was in receipt of a letter from the Company expressing their approval of our expense report and of my frugality.

"I'm glad the Company sees what I already know about you. In fact, I've been amiss in not mentioning I have been impressed with your understanding of numbers, budgets and such. You've a talent for it my love. If you weren't of such a lovely gender, I'd have you doing my books at the office! Hah! What a thought. I wouldn't get a lick of work out of the lads if you were wandering about."

I was very touched by his compliment for he was one to not say anything, rather than say something which was untrue.

Relieved the first party was over, I could now concentrate on my daily duties and spend some quiet time with wee Josie. Well, to call it 'quiet time' might be misleading. Her energy was boundless and her laughter infectious. Her curiosity was also unlimited, and I wondered if I would be able to be the one to answer her endless questions as she got older. These were just some of the thoughts rambling about in my head several weeks later as I went to the linen cupboard to get a clean shift. I as I did, my eyes glanced at the box I kept there for the cloths I used during my monthly courses. It seemed I hadn't used them for a while, but I had been so busy. I had to think back and try to recall my activities the last time I had and realized it was at least 5 weeks, or longer. My eyes opened wide and my mouth formed a silent O. I was expecting a child, our child. My heart jumped with the joyous thought of telling Thomas. There was no doubt in my mind he would be over the moon. He was such a wonderful Da to Josie and I know he's the type of man whose heart knows how to grow to encompass those he loves. And, another babe would not be a financial burden now.

Thomas came home in the evening with some work to do, but we almost always sat by the fire to talk of our day after a light supper. I asked Annie if she would put Josie to bed for me and I joined him just as he was pouring each of us a wee dram. He shared some events, including the arrival of a rare shipment of the much-desired spice called cloves. He handed me a small cloth packet from his pocket. I smelled it and found it extremely pleasant.

He said if I put this small sachet in with my clothing, they would always smell fresh and insects would be less likely to try to enter there. He also warned me the oil in cloves could leave a stain so to avoid letting them touch the material. I came over to him and thanked him for this lovely gift.

"Thomas, I have a gift for you also." I put my arm around his neck and settled myself upon his knees. His eyebrows raised and a smile brightened his face.

"My, my, darlin', you certainly caught my interest. What could you possibly have for me?"

I could tell by where his hand was wandering that he may have misinterpreted my intent.

Laughingly, I placed my hand over his to stop its progress, "Let's revisit your thought later. However, I have something else to share with you first. I believe God is going to bless us with a child in about seven months!"

Watching his face go from shock, to wonder, to joy was truly something to see! He wrapped his arms around me and rocked me back and forth as though I was the babe.

"Oh Fiona. What a wonderful surprise, what a grand gift. Won't Josie think she's quite the lady to be a 'big-sister'? We must write your parents this very night so it can go out on the Irish packet with the tide tomorrow. What do you think of Padraic for a name?"

Chuckling, "I think Padraic's a grand name, but don't you think we should see if it's a girl, or boy before we decide? Oh, and I think we should also write Lord and Lady Lynch too."

We went to bed in a euphoric mood and this time I gladly let his hands wander wherever they wanted to go.

A couple of days later, Thomas and I told Phoebe and Annie the news which brought broad smiles and congratulations. Then Thomas informed all of us he felt I should find a nanny to take over the extra work Annie had been doing for Josie. This would mean we would have someone well settled in by the time the child was born. As are most such posts filled in a household, Phoebe introduced us to one of her cousins. Jemma apparently had many years of experience with children of all ages. To be practical, I also interviewed a few others. One was too sour and too heavy. I couldn't see her being able to chase Josie about nor to have the patience needed with an active babe. One girl seemed very willing, but she was only thirteen and had no experience and the last one seemed too much enamored of the knick-knacks and possessions throughout the house. Jemma on the other hand, at about nineteen, seemed pleasant, intelligent and I liked the way she interacted with Josie. She listened and responded to her, yet I could see she would be firm with her. Of course, being Phoebe's cousin would also ensure she would not want to embarrass her family by failing to do her duty to my satisfaction. I explained she would have to share the work with Annie, so Josie didn't feel she was losing Annie as much as she is getting a new friend. They both agreed it was a good plan.

I also couldn't help but notice her dress and shoes were well kept, but extremely worn, I arbitrarily made a decision and informed her the position would require she wear a particular set of clothes which we would provide. She could hardly hide her pleasure. I knew Thomas would understand and agree.

The transition went smoothly, both women sorted out their responsibilities, all seemed to get along quite well. Josie was especially pleased by all of the extra attention. I could now concentrate on creating all the wee things a new babe would need. It was a pleasant task and I had more time to daydream about our new child.

SUMMER - 1603 ENGLAND

I think Thomas realized my time for leisure would be seriously limited once I've gave birth, for he has been taking Josie and me on little excursions when possible. He was teaching me to sail, which I also did in Kinsale, but usually with someone else at the helm. The fresh air seems to make my morning sickness a thing of little consequence and Josie loves being on the water. She squeals with delight when the spray comes over the sides and loves nothing better than to be held over the side so she can splash her pudgy little hands in the water. Her first birthday in July is upon us and now she is walking, and she loves to spend many hours exploring our garden on her stubby little legs. I often take her with me on errands as she loves to meet people and they are quite taken with her. She is beautiful with her stunning blue/green eyes and cascade of rich black curls. Her skin is unblemished and has a warm cast to it. I have taken to keeping her in bonnets when out of doors for I notice, instead of turning pink as I do in the sun, her skin starts to take on a golden hue.

One afternoon in September, I went to the pantry and found Annie sitting in the corner, quietly sobbing into her apron.

"Annie! What's wrong? Are you ill?'

"No, no Misses. Tis nothing."

"Come, come. It can't be nothing. Scottish lasses are not known for crying for naught, now are they?

With a nod and a sob, she explained.

"I've gotten word this morning me Mither is sore ill and the physicians say she may linger a while, but there's nae hope fer her. But, ye see, I understand such, for 'tis life, Aye? It's just I haven't seen her going nigh on seven years. I've meant to, but every time I've saved the fare, another brother, sister or cousin needed the money, and so it goes to Glasgow without me."

Sitting on the floor with her, I put my arm around this wee, strong woman and drew her to me when she starts weeping again. As I would expect from Annie, she soon snuffles and gathers herself together.

"Weel now. There's nae to be done about it, so I'll get aboot my chores and turn it over tae God, Aye? I thank ye for yer kindness and sympathy Missus"

She got up and left. I sat there and thought of how I would feel and immediately went to my desk and wrote a note to Thomas. I told him what all had transpired and explained I had no idea what the fare from Portsmouth to Glasgow might be, but if we could afford it, would he be willing to help our Annie go see her ailing mother. I asked Peter to take my note to Thomas right away and to wait for a reply. Within an hour he was back with reply in hand.

"Dearest Wife: The kindness of your heart is one of the many reasons I love you. My only concern is you will have one less person to help you around the house especially in your condition. However, if you feel this will not be a problem. I will leave word at the Post-House to request they make passage available as soon as Annie can leave, and the fare is to be billed to me. Also, please assure her she will not lose any wages during her absence for up to three weeks. Thank you for letting me know this. We have been so blessed it would be cruel to not use a small portion of it to relieve the pain of one who has been such an important part of our household. Your loving husband:"

I had tears in my eyes reading this and gratitude in my heart for this dear man. I called Annie into the library as soon as I could and shared the good news with her. Tears sprang to her eyes and bowing her head, she thanked us over and over again. I finally had to beg her to not act so for it was embarrassing me. Once she calmed down, I gave her the instructions she would need to book her fare and added one more bit of advice.

"Annie. I would ask one more thing of you regarding this. I prefer you not discuss the financial arrangements with anyone in the household, or even any one in town. Let it just be assumed you had the funds, or were able to get the funds, through your family. Tis no one's business and it would save Mr. Lydon and me some embarrassment. What we do is for your benefit and not for any praise, jealousy, or credit from others. Do you understand?"

"Aye ma'am I do. I will ne'er be able to thank you enough though. I shall light candles for you every day and will return as soon as I possibly can for, I have nae desire to take advantage of yer generosity. I will leave on the morrow, for I have little enough to pack and I believe it best to haste me home."

"That's grand Annie: And I will say prayers for your mother's strength, peace and faith she will enter God's kingdom with little discomfort and great joy. I will have Peter take you to the post-house right away to book the trip. Once you have the details, let me know and we will get word to your family by messenger. And remember, not a word about the money, not even to Peter."

She agreed, took two quick steps toward the hall, then abruptly turned back and gave me a very un-Annie like hug before running out. It took a few moments for my eyes to unblur.

Time went quickly with the extra work in Annie's absence and yet Josie, Thomas and I still seemed to find plenty of time together. Although, as summer lengthened, work demanded more time of Thomas including trips overseas and his absence was felt. I was fortunate Gennie made a habit of stopping by frequently and was such a delightful companion. It seemed we could walk about the garden and talk for hours. I could tell she missed home, but also, she truly loved her husband, despite his age and failing health. However, it was also obvious he adored and respected her. Nothing seemed to make him so content as to see her happy. One day she admitted one reason she liked to come over was so she could spend time with Josie. The two of them had grown quite close and the love which was developing was mutual. Although I never asked, she eventually brought up the subject of she and her husband not having any children.

"To be sure, tis a blessing I've prayed for but hasn't happened. We tried for many years and now my husband's health eliminates any chance."

I placed my hand upon her arm and made a sympathetic sound. She just patted my hand and went on.

"Whisht, don't fret. I have accepted it for what else can I do, eh? I relish my time with Josie, as I will your new babe and will continue to make a complete nuisance to my nieces and nephews. To tell the truth, being an Auntie is a grand job. I enjoy them, I spoil them and when they turn cranky or have soiled themselves, I go home," she laughed! "Oh, that reminds me! I have some fine news to share. I will be going home in September for a visit. Manfred's physician says he's responding well to the new tonic he's taking, and his sister has agreed to come care for him. I am most grateful. She's a dear woman, but I fear the thought of spending a long time with her does not appeal!"

"Oh, it certainly is good news, though I will miss you fiercely! September is at the end of the best sailing season. When will you return?"

"I'll be back well before you give birth. As long as I return before November, there will be some calm periods, so not to worry! I am quite giddy as a girl to see my boisterous family again."

"I shall be as fat as an old cow by the time you return and won't you just be feeling slim and fit, "I said warmly.

The additional chores turned out to be a blessing, for my heart was heavy saying farewell to my friend and a bit jealous she would be back in Ireland.

Annie returned as promised and I could see, despite the grief, it did her good to say her goodbyes in person.

One evening, Thomas was smiling like the cat who caught the canary. During supper he told me he had a surprise.

"I thought since you are not far along and seem to be doing well, we might do something very special." I have booked a trip to London and was able to get box tickets to see William Shakespeare's play, Much Ado About Nothing. I understand it is a wonderful comedy. I think it would be a terrible waste to be in England and not see both the city and one of his plays. What do you think?"

Oh my! What a surprise! I must admit I was torn between joy and trepidation. I had heard London was amazingly large, and I could hardly catch my breath to think of seeing such a sight. However, the opportunity to see a play would be worth it. I calmed a bit when I realized Thomas was familiar with such things and would never put me in harm's way. Therefore, I hugged him soundly and told him he surely must be the kindest husband ever. We would go the following week and I was well packed upon departure.

The trip was fairly comfortable, with frequent rest stops. I was surprised at the comparatively short distance between each hamlet and how well the road was maintained. However, not too terribly far from our destination, I started to notice a foul odor in the air. Since my nose seemed to be overly sensitive of late, I didn't mention it to Thomas, but peered about out the window to see if I could identify the source. The stench soon got stronger and Thomas noticed me holding my kerchief to my nose.

"Fiona. I am so sorry. I should have warned you. This reek happens to be your first introduction to London. There are so many people living in the city there's really no way to prevent the smell and it is always worse in hot weather. I will buy you a pomander when we arrive. They sell them everywhere. The oranges with clove and cinnamon are the best. Believe it or not, you will get a little used to it after a while."

"That's good to know. However, please ask the coachman to pull over immediately as I am going to be quite ill right now."

After such an unpleasant introduction, I did have a wonderful time. We stayed in a delightful public residence quite near the Tower of London, took a boat down the Thames and I was completely enthralled by the play. Our private box gave us a complete view of the stage and I could hear every word. It was also a treat to see the members of royalty in their very well-appointed boxes. By their actions, clothing and banter, I sensed they were there more to be seen than to see. Some of the goings on rivaled the scenes on stage and led me to believe they didn't realize a 'private box' did not offer the level of privacy they required! Exhausted, but happy, I slept most of the way home and had the stuff of daydreams for the rest of my life.

I am spending most of the long end of summer days with Josie while the household staff puts the gardens to bed. It is peaceful work which is easy for me to do despite my condition. Annie keeps an eagle eye out for me to ensure I don't overdo and is the first to call Peter to come help with moving soil and removing cuttings. By the end of October, the morning fog lingers and there are only a few hours of real sunshine, so our time outside is limited. On one of the rare, warmer days, I am trimming some rose bushes and notice a pain in my lower back. I had been leaning over quite a bit, so I decided to do some trimming from a sitting position. Unfortunately, a shadow of discomfort lingered and worsened. I feel it best to go lie down. Walking carefully, I lay down on the chaise in the sunroom and called for Annie.

"Sorry to bother you Annie, but would you get me a hot cloth to place under my back. I fear I've pulled at a muscle."

"Right away Missus, and I'll bring some water."

I lay as still as I could, but the discomfort lingered. She soon returned and slid a flat hot stone wrapped in flannel under my back and it eased the pain almost immediately. I sipped my water, thanked Annie and semi-dozed as the heat did its work. It was only moments though before the pain came back and increased. I felt a strong urge to get up and move about even though it seemed smarter to be still. I finally gave into it and it appeared to alleviate the pain. Then, suddenly, I felt as though someone had gripped my innards with burning tongs. I remember screaming and feeling a hot gush between my legs, then a black void.

I awakened, confused to be in bed while it was light outside. Thomas was holding my hand and I slowly looked him, but not understanding why he was there. I had never seen such anguish on his face before and it was swollen from crying.

"Thomas! What's wrong my love?"

He opened his mouth but couldn't speak. A memory flashed, then another and my mind recalled the pain. I then knew our babe was lost. Gasping with awareness, Thomas pulled me close to him and we wept together.

The physician made me stay abed as my bleeding was long and heavy, Thomas went about the miserable business of properly sending off such a wee soul. He came to sit with me often, but we had little to say. Those little daily tidbits we shared suddenly seemed mundane and unimportant. We did try to keep our spirits up around Josie and were relieved when she stopped asking the whereabouts of the babe we told her was coming. "She's (for it was a girl) with God in Heaven." was finally accepted as a reasonable explanation and Jemma kept her occupied when we were unable to face her. As happens in all death, life went on and we went about our business. I soon sensed from friends and acquaintances that those who have never lost a child before its birth, feels it's not the same; not as meaningful; not as painful as losing a child born. They don't realize there is a hole in your being which you cannot fill. A promise unsatisfied. A child you never got to know.

Thomas has been spending longer hours at work and bringing more work home. The quiet time we used to enjoy is now just a quiet time, with Thomas at his desk and me at my mending or reading. I force myself to pretend enjoyment as I read to Josie or listen to her prattle on about her dollies, butterflies and such, but it is an act. For a while after the death, I looked forward to falling into the dark abyss of sleep. But now I enter an arena of bleak dreams and self-recriminations. My feelings of deceit and guilt come creeping back like a thief who has simply been hiding in a dark corner. The horror of the attack replays itself again and I see Josie and Thomas turning from me as if I were a leper. It is clear to me the loss of this child is, again, my punishment and now made even worse by punishing Thomas for something of which he isn't guilty. As he copes with his grief, he tries to be kinder to me in mine. However, his thoughtfulness grates on me. It reminds me I am unworthy. It magnifies my inability to be kind to him. I do just the opposite. I cry because I am homesick and blame it on him. I am sharp and critical.

"You made me come to this country full of people who look down on us. You made me leave kith and kin all for your need to be more important, for your own ambitions."

"Would you rather I had stayed and continued making a pittance in Kinsale, depending upon the charity of your parents? Perhaps you miss the minimal food available even months after the battles, or wish we were living in the wee stone house, working for hours on your hands and knees trying to coax vegetables from a tiny garden. You wouldn't have the time, or energy, to be so bitter, so homesick if you didn't neglect Josie so. We have lost one child and you are trying to lose the other! Why don't you try to be grateful for what we have and be a proper mother and mistress of a home others would give anything to have."

He storms out of the room as I break down in tears. I am lost. I want to go home. I want to fill this hole in my heart by going back to before; to where I was surrounded by my family, instead of cold-hearted strangers; to before ugliness entered my soul and took my innocence, before God took my child ere I ever knew her, before Thomas hated me. I now understood the meaning of the word desolation.

However, slowly each day, each mundane task, each responsibility I had to take care of made it a bit easier to do the next. Instead of avoiding spending time with Josie, dreading the reminder of one missing from the nursery, I am rediscovering my joy in her. She has magically gone from incomprehensible babbling to actual communication. My smile has quietly snuck back and I'm learning to stifle the guilt I feel in little pleasures even though a precious part of Thomas and me lays cold in the ground. I turned back to God and the church, instead of sitting through Mass filled with anger at Him. By the time Gennie comes home, (Oh I was never so glad to see someone!) I can talk about the loss and I let her sympathy pour over me like a balm. She lets me know the pain will lessen but the scar will never go away and this is as it should be so her soul would always be remembered.

However, Thomas and I have not seemed to be able bring ourselves back to each other. He stays busier than ever with his work, whether at the office or at home and I stay busy with required dinners held and dinners attended. When we sit together, it seems we struggle to discuss anything but household events. Personal, intimate questions die on our lips before we can speak them. We dance around the void which has grown, and we can't find a bridge on which to cross it. Thomas sleeps in his room and seldom crosses the threshold into mine. When he does, our embraces are more designed to accomplish a purpose, rather than to make love. I feel less fulfilled after than before he joins me, and I can tell he feels the same.

One Sunday afternoon while doing books and correspondence in the library, Jemma rushed in.

"Missus, Josie isn't waking well from her nap. She feels quite warm and like she's still half asleep."

I ran to her bedside I could tell immediately she was flushed, and her half-opened eyes were overly bright. "Jemma, quickly, bring me a bowl of cool water and some cloths. Oh, and a cup of water."

I sat for almost an hour trying to cool her down and couldn't get her to take even a sip of water. She slipped deeper and deeper into sleep. I sent Peter on his way to fetch the physician. Thomas was at a church meeting and I asked Peter to have him come home. I forced myself to concentrate on changing the damp cloths, but I was sick with fear. Other than unhealthy red blossoms on her cheeks, her face was pale and sweaty, and her sweet little limbs were as limp as a doll's.

The physician arrived quickly and was examining her when Thomas arrived. All we could do was stand quietly waiting for his conclusions. I nervously fingered my rosary and the prayers I was trying to recite were all muddled in my head. The only thing I could keep repeating over and over was, "Dear God, please don't take her. We will not survive another loss."

Thomas slipped his hand in mine and we stood shoulder to shoulder supporting each other.

Finally, the physician stood up and addressed us, "Your instincts were right Mrs. Lydon. The damp, cool cloths are exactly what I recommend. In fact, there's not much more to be done at this point. If the fever cannot be cooled, it will not end well. Our bodies, especially of a child, cannot abide it. She will need constant cooling and try to drip water into her mouth a drop or two at a time. Don't attempt to give her much as she may choke. If she improves you may add broth, but at this point, use water only. Even though it seems wrong, because she is so hot, keep her covered so she doesn't get chilled. Be sure to send someone for me should you see any kind of a rash, a rigidity of her limbs, or a violent thrashing."

Those last words almost did me in. I had seen too many children buried in my family and those of others to not take his admonitions seriously.

Standing, the good Physician put his hand on Thomas's shoulder, "I'm sorry. There's nothing else I can do. Her life is in God's hands."

He left and Thomas and I held each other as our tears came, then we knelt, saying our Rosary and praying fervently for Josie's recovery. I gave Annie instructions to keep Josie's room supplied with cool water and cloths. I adamantly told Thomas I would be the one to care for Josie, and he should return to his office to take care of pressing business. He could come back earlier than usual if he wanted and bring his work with him, for I knew he was overwhelmed at this time of year. He tried to argue with me, but I wouldn't listen. He promised to return as soon as possible, kissed my forehead and left.

I wrapped Josie in some fresh linen, held her on my lap and applied the damp cloths to her hot forehead and behind her neck as the physician had shown us. The heat rose off her like a stove and the cloths turned warm within minutes. I talked to her and sang. I told her some of her favorite tales. I could only pray she heard me for only the presence of the fever gave any indication she had any life in her. When I grew silent my mind immediately filled with the familiar self-recrimination and fear. I tried to stem the tears for I knew I needed to be strong. Again, I fell into an icy depth of belief that I had brought this punishment upon us; therefore, I should be the only one to nurse our little one back to health. Annie and Phoebe continued to bring cooled water and a small bit for me to eat, even though I had no appetite. In their goodness, they encouraged me and told me I must stay strong for Josie's sake. Thomas came home early and was distraught about Josie having not improved at all. He insisted he take over the nursing tasks, despite my arguments. I gave in and took the time to freshen up, have some broth and lay down but sleep eluded me. I'm back within the hour, pushing Thomas away, changing her linens again and repeating the continual use of the cooling cloths. Thomas reluctantly goes downstairs. Annie says she saw him in the parlor kneeling in prayer and saying his Rosary.

This went on for two days while I cared for her. She swallowed some drops of water and her fever seemed to abate only to come back like fury in a few hours, so hot she could hardly be touched. She thrashed and moaned yet didn't awaken. I found whispering and singing to her seemed to calm her and gave her a little peace. Thomas begged me to please let him help but I wouldn't hear of it. I told him I was fine as I can sup as easily in the chair as not, and I can drift off for a brief sleep when she is still.

The third morning, just before dawn, Thomas softly approached me while I slept; took Josie gently from my arms and placed her in her little bed. He carried me to our bed, laid me down and covered me against the morning chill. He then went to Josie, changed her gown and took my place at the chair by the window. Completely unaware of this I slept for nine hours straight while he cared for our daughter as gently as one might care for a wee kitten. Just as evening came on, Thomas awakened me by crying out in alarm and ran to the bedside with Josie. She was shivering something fierce and sweat poured off her, soaking her gown and Thomas's chest.

" Fi! Fi! Wake up. Oh, Holy Mother, help us."

The look of terror on his face is something I never wanted to see again. I reached for her and tucked her into the warm nest where I had been laying and started wiping her down. After about a half of an hour she stopped shaking and sweating as suddenly as if a candle had been blown out. Her temperature started dropping and I cried out. I was sure we had lost her. Thomas picked her up and held her chest to his ear.

"Her heart's beating Fi and I can feel her breath upon my cheek. Take her back in your arms and keep her warm while I send for the physician. I won't be long."

By the time the physician came Josie, pale but cool, was sleeping restfully with her little thumb stuffed in her mouth and curled up like a puppy. The physician found Thomas and me sobbing in each other's arms for this miracle. I don't think either of us got more than a few hours' sleep all night as we constantly checked on her. However, we did spend much of the time talking, crying, reminiscing and starting our journey to find our way back to the love we held for each other.
One would never have known Josie was so close to death. Every day was a gift.

PEACE, PLANS AND PLOTS - 1607

Months turned into years and before we knew it, Josie was five and we were caught up in celebrating yet another Christmas. We got so much joy out of Josie's wonder at the candles, songs, sweet treats and decorative greenery throughout the house. She and I took great pleasure in using the frosted windows to practice the letters she had learned in the hornbook tied at her little waist. She was such a quick little imp and could already pick out a few words in the wooden book her father made for her. There were only sporadic days of light snow in Portsmouth, which meant there would be little sledding and snow forts, but the land was so flat it wouldn't have been the same as riding the thrilling hill sides in Kinsale! However, the sharp winds off the water left no doubt we were in the grip of Father Winter, so we were most happy when we were finally able to welcome spring. It made my heart sing to see the flower's colors burst forth and increase daily as I gazed through the diamond panes. The bubbles and imperfections in the glass made it seem as though I was viewing the garden from underwater.

As the weather warmed, we walked in the garden and I would point out the different plants and herbs to Josie. Oddly, without any particular reason why, we had recently shortened her name to Jo! She was already starting to understand if we were upset with her, it was Josephine; if we were being serious with her, it was Josie, and if all was right with her world, it was Jo.

Thomas was a content man. His wife and daughter loved him, his home was more comfortable and peaceful than he ever could have dreamed and his position as manager had opened a door on the world and a view of events unfolding around us. More and more people talked of the New World across the Atlantic. Different countries were planning and plotting ways to take advantage of possible riches and lands. At supper, Thomas spoke at length about these changes and what it might mean in the long run.

"I think England has finally realized she needs to take the New World seriously! Spain is well ahead of us with her claims on lands and riches in New Spain and the Caribbean Islands. The lands there experience warm climes year-round which means continual planting and harvesting! They have sugar plantations which make huge amounts of money because the labor is all done by slaves or aborigines who are paid almost nothing! France is trying to make inroads in the northern areas, but they aren't doing so well. I think their coffers are quite slim after their many wars and the weather in the north is not as hospitable as the Spanish lands. There are many rumors, and some quite solid, of England getting charters, and starting companies like the East India Company, to claim and settle the eastern coast there. I have heard the land is exceptionally fertile and sparsely settled."

"Why would Englishmen want to risk leaving hearth and home for a wilderness? I believe I have heard there is no promise of gold and silver there as it was in the Spaniard's conquests and it is populated with savages."

"I know. Quite a risk to be sure. But our system here is changing too. The Lords of various manors and lands have almost always left most, if not all, of their estate to the eldest son. Then the younger ones sustained themselves through military service, squiring etc. Well Fi, it is not working anymore. Gadding about in dashing uniforms and fighting for various governments just isn't lucrative these days. The aristocrats tried to resolve the issue by dividing their lands amongst more of the sons. But one can only divide so much before no one is doing well. Why what would we do if Jo married the youngest son of some Lord of the Manor? They would end up living in genteel poverty! Ireland has certainly proven surviving off half-starved tenant farmers isn't the answer either. We need strong, young adventurous men to open up new lands in the name of the King, to be followed by more of the same."

"Do you think such a venture would be successful and we might live long enough to see such a thing?"

"Yes! Absolutely. I have heard they are hoping to have one colony, or more, started by 1610. Just think Fi, perhaps we might even go there someday. We're both young and if I'm still with the Company, I may even be sent there."

I wasn't too sure such an idea appealed to me, but Thomas's enthusiasm was hard to resist.

Jo was now in a neighborhood school for girls. At almost 6 years, her mind was always going as fast as a loom and I couldn't keep her occupied enough to keep her out of mischief. She loved her new school and came home full of information and chatter. She could hardly wait to impress her Da at supper with the latest lessons. I did spend some extra time with her on arithmetic and history as it seems the ladies at the school did not find either subject of much value to girls beyond the simplest applications.

Our latest news from home was welcome. But it wasn't all good either. My Da's health was failing and Mam was feeling the years too. Both Robbie and Colum were married and starting families of their own. I also wanted to make sure Chloe, always so generous with her time by helping Mam run the household, would not have to stretch the pennies. She was sacrificing enough by staying home. It seems Mick was showing an interest in courting her. Her friendship with the lad was blossoming into something more, but her responsibilities put a damper on what should have been carefree and romantic days. Thomas and I would spend an evening a month going over our household finances and were always able to find some extra to send home.

On Tuesday, one of those bright late spring days when the sun sparkled off the water and the sounds from the busy port drifted through the windows on a soft breeze, started well. I was at my secretary working on some household lists when I heard a carriage coming up the drive at a gallop. Jumping up, I was at the door by the time the horses pulled up in a spray of gravel. Two men leapt down and assisted another from inside the coach. My heart stopped when I saw they were lifting Thomas from the seat to carry him inside. His head was bloodied, and he was unconscious. I stepped back and directed them to a sofa. Amos, the one I recognized as an employee from the office, answered the unasked questions on my face.

"Miz Lydon, we've sent for the physician. Mister Lydon was on the quay when a runaway horse and cart ran into him. There was no way he could get out of the way! His head hit the boulders on the roadside and the heavily laden cart ran over his legs. I'm so sorry. We thought it best to bring him here right away."

"Yes, yes of course." As they lay him down, I quickly folded my thick shawl to place under his head. That was when I saw his right leg bent at an angle in which it was never meant to be. The room suddenly swayed around me and only the quick thinking of one of men kept me from ending up on the floor. Annie was by my side in moments with a glass of port. I sat on the footstool with Thomas's cold hand in mine as we waited for the physician. His face couldn't be described as anything but gray as clay and I instructed the men to go to the office and let them know what happened and to ask Henry Bell to come to the house. Just moments after they left, the physician arrived. He spent much time going over the wounds. When he cut the cloth away from Thomas's legs it was even worse than it looked, not just for ragged lacerations but it was obvious there was at least one break in the left one and a bloody end of a bone was sticking out of the skin on the right.

"God's blood! The cart must have been laden with stones. As concerned as I am that Thomas has not regained consciousness, it will be a blessing when I reset the bones."

He had me ask Annie to cover Thomas with a warm blanket and to ask Peter to come help him with the bone-setting.

"Peter be careful to not jostle his head. Lay your upper body over his shoulders and hold his arms. This is not going to be pleasant and probably will bring him around with a start."

Putting pressure on the top portion of Thomas's thigh the physician grabbed the bone just above the knee, jerked it down and twisted it before letting go. Thomas jerked, gasped and moaned, but did not awaken. I could hear the physician let out his breath.

"Now," he said, "The lower leg will be more difficult. There are two bones, both are broken, but the smaller is protruding through the skin. Madam, would you be good enough to give me a portion of strong liquor and a towel?"

I did so and the physician placed the towel under the lower leg, poured about half of the liquor over the open wound and drank the rest down in one gulp. He grabbed the bones, pulling the lower portion until it receded back into the leg and twisted the two ends until they seemed to align. Thomas barely moaned but turned as white as a ghost. The sound of the bones grinding was excruciatingly loud in the quiet room. I barely made it out the front door before my stomach emptied.

The physician placed and wrapped splints the full length of the leg, cleansed the various wounds, paying special attention to the head wound. Peter brought him a plank where they placed him carefully and they carried him up to a spare bedroom. He then asked to speak with me.

"My dear, I must be honest with you for it would only be cruel not to. Thomas's legs may heal. However, they are quite damaged and will never be as strong, nor as straight as they were. Also, the open wound is at greatest risk of inflammation, or even a festering which might require amputation, or possibly cause death. It must be kept as clean as possible with frequent changing of the bandages. I will come by frequently to check it. Now, be as it may, I am more concerned with his head wound. Since he suffered though my ministrations and such pain without regaining consciousness is not a good sign. There is little we can do to determine the outcome. He may simply wake up in a few days and suffer no more than headaches. He may wake up but not be right in the head. He might lose his memory or succumb to various levels of madness. He may not wake up at all and simply slip away."

His words were entering my mind slowly, like individual drops of water while I tried to absorb them. I couldn't imagine my energetic, quick-witted Thomas wasting away. It felt like someone just drew a black cloth over the door to our future. There were no decisions to be made together, no new plans. There was just a void. I didn't cry or speak. I felt paralyzed. The physician stood, placed his hand on my shoulder and said he would be back in a few days and to send for him if there were any changes. I sat in a daze by Thomas's bedside for almost an hour, just watching his chest rise and fall and not thinking at all.

This is how Annie found me when she announced Henry Bell was downstairs. She had to repeat this a few times before I understood.

"Oh? Yes. Send him up. I'll speak to him here."

Henry dashed into the room, took one look at Thomas's inert body, covered in bandages, and had to grasp the bedpost to remain upright.

"Oh, sweet Jesus, Fiona! The lads said he was seriously injured, but I had no idea. Are both legs hurt then? Is he in terrible pain?"

"Yes. Both have been seriously damaged. He's not feeling the pain now, but it appears to be a blessing and a curse. He is insensible and the physician can give no assurances of his coming back to us, when, or if he will be of sound mind if he does. All we can do now is pray, care for his body and trust it will heal."

Reaching for my hand he whispered, "Oh dear lady, I am so sorry for your troubles, although I am somewhat relieved Thomas is not suffering right now as I would think the pain would be nearly unbearable. What can I do for you?"

"Oh, nothing Henry. I can barely think right now. Every time I start to, I end up at a dead-end and must try to go a different direction. Wait! I really should see to Jo. She must be so confused and afraid. Would you sit with him while I am gone? I can't bear the thought of him being alone."

He reassured me it was no problem and for me to take care of whatever was needed.

Gratefully, I left the room and found wee Jo in the kitchen in front of a plate of uneaten bread and jam. I was so glad I came for she had tears shimmering on her dark lashes and she ran to my arms when she saw me. I tried to explain the accident by reminding her she was very,

very sick a while back and she got better, and we would pray her Da would too.

"What about my baby sister? She didn't get better and now she's in the church yard. I don't want Da to go there."

She broke down in sobs and all I could do was hold her for I didn't want to make promises I couldn't keep. All I could do was comfort her. I took her to her room and tucked her in with her favorite doll, Gingerbread. As children do, she eventually closed her eyes and slept. I envied her the respite.

I freshened up and brought some ale and buttered bread upstairs for Henry and me. I had learned from the past it would be wise to take care of myself so I might take care of my dear husband. Henry said there had been no change for better, or for worse. We sat together in silence for a bit when Henry turned to me.

"Fiona. I have been thinking while you were with Jo, and I believe we have to discuss some plans before others discover the extent of Thomas's injuries. I'm not sure if you are aware this situation could cause some other serious problems."

"Cause some other problems! Of course, this will cause problems. We have no idea right now if Thomas will live or die, or if he lives, if he will be able to function. This is the main problem right now. We have no idea what's going to happen. Surely you must see that Henry."

"My God Fiona. Of course, I know it is what is of most importance now. However, I am thinking in terms of the near future and in faith that Thomas will recover.

We must protect what he has worked so hard to accomplish here and we must consider the Seven Year agreement in Thomas's contract with the Company."

I just looked at him blankly. What could he be talking about?

Oh dear! I can see by the look on your face you have no idea to what I'm referring. Well, it cannot wait. We must discuss this now. Let me explain and you will see how much this could affect you and Jo's future. Of course, Thomas draws a very comfortable salary, household allowance and a percentage of profit while he holds his current position. Which is all well and good. However, there is a clause which states, to ensure one of those benefits, he is required to work for them for a full seven years before leaving the company. In order to give him an incentive to do so, he had to agree to waive his rights to his percentage of the profits should he leave their employ before he has met the seven-year commitment. I don't have the timeline, or the figures off the top of my head, but I'm pretty sure he still has at least a year and a half to go to keep the agreement intact. Unfortunately, such restriction would also stand should, God forbid, he does not recover."

"Oh Henry! Do you really think the company would hold this over us if he should die from this tragic accident while in their employ? They have always seemed to have thought very highly of him and surely they must know he has always kept their best interests at heart."

"Most certainly so. But you must not mistake their personal feelings for Thomas as something they would put over their concern regarding the profit margin of the company. I dislike having to discuss this with you at this time, but we must consider it is necessary to keep the extent of his injuries unknown while ensuring the management of the business in Portsmouth is kept on an even keel while we wait to see how he fares. Since the owners are all in London, they would not be aware of Thomas's actual condition unless someone told them. In this instance the someone I am most concerned about would be Stanley Haverstead. Nothing would thrill him more than to advise the board of Thomas's inability to manage the Portsmouth office and of course he would put himself forth as the perfect man for the job. "

"Wait. Wouldn't the job go to you since I know Thomas has spoken on a number of occasions that the job of manager should eventually go to you? He has made it clear privately and publicly he feels you would be the right person for the position."

"You would certainly think so, except Stanley has the power through family ties, his petty personality and his underhandedness to make sure I would not be chosen. I trust you understand my job is not my main concern. I can always find employment elsewhere with my background. I am concerned you and your daughter would not be cared for in the manner Thomas had planned and I'm sure Stanley would not show you the consideration of letting you stay in your home during any lengthy convalescence."

"What can we do Henry? Unless Thomas is visited by an Angel of miracles in the next day or two, it is unlikely we can keep this a secret."

"I may have a plan, but I need to go back to the office to consider the workability of it and my first step will be to inform the employees of a more positive picture of the likelihood Thomas will recover. I think I will stop at the physician's office on my way to ask him to not divulge the seriousness of these injuries, especially the head injury. I will then get a message to headquarters post haste to advise them of Thomas's injuries, but not the extent of the them. May I come back this evening so we can discuss the possibility of my ideas working?"

We agreed to meet in the evening, and I stayed busy arranging with the household how we would care for Thomas. At least Henry gave me a glimmer of hope after the cruel news that this horrendous accident could be even worse than I feared.

Henry arrived as planned in the evening bearing a large satchel of documents and ledgers. We sat head to head for several hours going through his plans to prevent both of our futures from being destroyed. When we were done, I looked at him in amazement and could most certainly see why Thomas trusted this young man to be the one to take over his post. It would require dedication on both of our parts and a lot of extra work, but there was no doubt we were willing to do this. Unfortunately, none of this would help if Thomas didn't eventually recover, but it might give us the time we and Thomas needed.

This is how it would work. Other than ourselves and our household staff, who would rather die than divulge information they were asked not to, no one was to know Thomas's mental condition. Henry was very aware I often helped my husband with his work and had a good head for figures. Therefore, he would bring work here in the evening and I would concentrate on the ledgers, etc. and Henry would concentrate on correspondence, which required language skills I did not have. He would try to get as much done at the office as possible and if I needed his help on a task, I was to send Peter with a message regarding the issue. We would advise others that the doctor did not want visitors for fear of corruption of his healing wounds and to avoid exhaustion. Henry even thought of a way to get Stanley out of the office for he would surely try to create havoc while Thomas was away. He was going to send Stanley on a trip to Holland allegedly to negotiate some new shipping arrangements. Unknown to Stanley, Henry was going to send a letter in advance to our agent in Holland advising them of limitations which would be in place in order to make these negotiations difficult and lengthy. He reassured the recipient of this letter that his assistance in making sure Mr. Haverstead's efforts failed would most assuredly bear fruit in their future private dealings. We admitted to each other we knew we couldn't play this game for an extended period for Thomas could not last very long if he was unable to take food and water. However, the plan certainly gave us an opportunity to prevent Stanly from prematurely jeopardizing our plans. We agreed to meet again in two days to finish the work Henry was leaving with me and to get started on whatever was next.

When he arrived as planned, I met Henry as soon as he was shown into the library. Stepping forward I took his hands and with joy written all over my face I shared some the good news. Just about an hour or two before, Thomas opened his eyes.

"Henry, isn't this wonderful? He seemed understandably confused but was able to sip some watered ale. Peter went immediately to fetch the physician. He's upstairs examining him now. This may not be as bleak as we feared."

"Good news indeed! And, assuming it will still take him quite a while to make headway, we can still to go forward with our plan until such time as there is no need."

We both turned as the physician entered the room.

"I must admit this sudden change is a sign of hope. He couldn't have lasted for too long as he was. Remember though, this is only one step on a long journey. I know he appears to be awake, but it is really more like one experiencing sleepwalking. He can take food and drink, be dressed, be kept clean etc. But he can do none of it himself. He's not really aware of what he hears or sees. He will feel pain now and will moan with it, but if you try to ask him questions, or instruct him to take an action on his own, he will not comprehend the request. He is very much like as infant"

Seeing both of our faces fall, he quickly explained there was a chance he could regain his faculties in time. We would hold onto such hope for it was a lifeline we were willing to reach for.

The next day dawned with a new routine and less darkness. Thomas was in truth no longer in a sleeping state, but as warned, he was also not quite in the present either. The tasks needed to care for him were difficult and disjointed at the beginning, but we quickly learned to work as a team. The entire household, the physician and Henry embraced this challenge with a desire to help this loving, decent and hardworking man. Although I was doing many of the jobs I did when Jo was so ill, I now needed Peter to help me move Thomas to change bed linens and such. We discovered if we propped him up on pillows, he would automatically swallow when liquid's such as broth were placed in his mouth. It was time consuming but at least we knew he was getting the food he needed to grow stronger. He didn't resist when we had to move him, even though we could hear he was in pain. The wounds on his legs which had become red and inflamed at first, eventually started healing, although it was obvious the bones did not look the same as before. He was losing weight and it was easy to see he was also losing strength in his limbs. Fortunately, Peter came up with an idea and the physician said he didn't see how it could hurt. Peter would come up twice a day and work Thomas's arms and legs. He said such exercises should strengthen them for he had often used those movements to help animals who had been hurt and weren't able to walk around while they healed. This idea sounded quite clever to me and it made the possibility of his recovery more real.

Every so often someone would come by for a visit, to bring flowers or a special dish. We thanked them warmly and always advised them Thomas had just gone down for a nap or was in consultation with an important client. After our plan had been in place for a week, or so, we were feeling much more confident about it and I would share it with Thomas, even though he couldn't really hear me. I just felt it was important to keep talking to him. Henry felt the same way. He started getting some correspondence back from Stanley and from his coconspirator in Holland which he would share with Thomas. He said Thomas would have roared at hearing about Stanley trying to be a sly negotiator and getting nowhere!

"Annie? Are you going out to market this morning?"

"Aye. Did ye need something special?"

"It's such a fine day I thought I'd take Jo out. She's getting restless and bothered by her Da's illness. Since I have to go to the apothecary to pick up the salve for Thomas's skin, I thought I'd have Peter take us down to the docks and we could do our shopping while he went to the office for messages. It would save you a lengthy walk and would give me company."

"A fine idea to be sure! Let me fetch me cloak and basket, aye?"

It truly was a lovely day with warm sunshine and a cool breeze blowing from the south. Jo was glued to the carriage's window taking in the sights.

Reaching over and hugging me she asked, "Will you buy me a sweet, Mam?

"I will if you'll be good and stay right by my side!"

Peter quickly had us at the top of the street where the merchants sold an amazing assortments of food stuffs from all around the world.

"Peter! Let us out here and we'll shop along the way. The apothecary's is at the end of the street and we'll meet you there."

I hadn't realized how long it had been since I had been shopping for myself. The displays of dried fruits, nuts and cheeses were amazing. Annie, Jo and I both took advantage of the little nibbles the merchants gave out to entice us to buy their wares. Of course, Jo wanted to buy the first sweet she saw but I made her wait until she had seen all she could choose from. She finally settled on a sweet bun with a date in the center covered in a fine layer of sugar. I told her she must keep it in the paper wrapping until we were on our ride home, so she didn't get the sticky coating all over her. Annie was soon done with fulfilling her list and we started a leisurely stroll toward the end of the street and on to my errand.

About halfway down I noticed a beggar sitting against the wall and instinctively moved Jo to the side of me farthest away from the man. He was really in a bad way. His clothes were obviously those of a seaman, but they were barely more than tattered rags. The man's hair and beard were severely matted, and he had open sores on his legs. His feet were so black it took me a moment to realize he wasn't wearing shoes. I couldn't help but feel sorry for the wretch, so I reached into the purse at my waist and pulled out a couple of small coins. As I passed him, I dropped them into his outstretched, scrawny, hand, being careful not to touch him. Instinctively, though I glanced at him and our eyes met, just for a quick moment. Looking away quickly I continued walking. I hadn't gone four steps before I stopped cold. It was him! No, it couldn't be. With a jerk I looked over my shoulder and the man was looking at me, his head tilted with a quizzical expression on his face. My stomach clenched and grasping Jo closer to me I started walking away as quickly as I could.

Poor little Jo cried out, "Mam! Mam, you're hurting me!"

Mumbling my apologies, I loosened my grip but did not slow my pace. How could this be? That Spaniard. That defiler of women. That mean, cruel, evil man was here and much too near me. I didn't look back again for there was always hope he did not recognize me, but I did not want to give him a chance to do so. By now we were at the apothecary and I darted in the door. Annie, out of breath, followed on my heels.

"Tell me Missus. What's wrong? Ye was moving as though the devil hisself was after ye. Oh, sweet Mary, your face has turned white."

She was right. I was as shaky as a newborn lamb. I had to think fast to give her a reason and felt the closer I stayed to the truth, without divulging my secret, the better it would be.

"Annie, did you see the beggar on the street? Well, he said some frightening things to me, and I was afraid he was going to try to grab me. Of course, it gave me quite a scare. Would you do me a favor and look out on the street to see if he is still where he was sitting? "

"Aye. Tis no trouble. You and the lass stay here behind these crates."

In just a moment Annie dashed back and told me the beggar was standing only two doors up and looking around. She said Jo and I should just stay where we were for, we couldn't be seen from the doorway. She would go to the clerk and get the salve I needed. I agreed and was glad to have the creates to lean against as my head was in a whirl. Annie was back in a trice with the purchase and told me the clerk said we could leave by the back entrance and could not be seen from the street. Once I was sure we were safe, we dashed out the back and found a good spot to watch for Peter. Annie checked again and said the beggar was back to where I had seen him at first. I could tell Jo sensed something was amiss for she was as quiet as a little mouse. Fortunately, Peter showed up and I told Annie to not tell him of the incident, for I had probably let my imagination get the best of me.

I covered my hands with my skirts on the way home to hide my trembling. What if he did recognize me? I tried to reassure myself he would have no way of knowing my name, nor the likelihood of questioning anyone who would. Would he have gotten a good enough look to recognize me, or worse yet close enough to Jo to recognize those rich black curls so similar to his?

I threw myself into my duties upon my return home and slept poorly, plagued by disturbing nightmares. I lost interest in food and had a hard time concentrating on mundane tasks. I spent more time with Thomas for I found I felt calmer when he was near.

Just a few days after my encounter with the filthy Spaniard, while reading by Thomas's bedside, I dozed off and dreamt…. I see Thomas is in his bed but there is a rock wall between us.

He turned his face toward me and said "Fiona! Come here. I love you and I need you." I ran toward him, but the wall was in my way. No matter how hard I scrambled and reached, I couldn't climb the wall to get over it.

I cried out, "I can't Thomas. I can't get past the wall. I want to, but I cannot." Then, to my amazement, I reached in my apron pocket and placed another stone on the wall. I didn't want to do it, but I could not help myself. I sat at the base of the wall with my head bowed and my hands around my knees and sobbed. Suddenly I sensed someone next to me. I looked up and there was an old farmer standing next to me with a stone in his hand.

"Eh! Why do ye keen so lass?"

"It's the wall," I cried. "My husband has need of me and I cannot reach him."

"Weel Dearie, it's what walls are for, aye? They are either there to protect the one on the other side, or to protect ye from the one on the other side. Now it's a foine wall and it seems to me ye've only two choices. Ye can continue making the wall stronger and try to take comfort in its protection, or ye can tear it down."

"I cannot. I cannot. I'm not strong enough."

The farmer then handed me the stone he was holding and smiling kindly, said, "Ye are that strong miss. Ye are strong enough to keep adding to the wall and ye are strong enough to tear it down. Either one will be difficult. Ye must decide which will give ye peace and accomplish what yer heart really wants."

"What if I tear down the wall and Thomas is no longer there, or he no longer wants me?"

The old farmer simply looked down at me, smiled, shrugged his shoulders and walked off into a mist.

I awoke with a start and looked toward Thomas, still and quiet in his false slumber. I could almost see the stone wall as it was in my dream. I knew what I must do. I put my work aside and moved my chair to his bedside and took his hand in mine. Its warmth always surprised me for it was so pale and still, I felt it should be cold. Looking closely at his long dark lashes upon his pale cheeks, the very sweetness of his mouth, I realized I could finally tell my secret to my dear husband. I knew I was safe for he would not and could not judge me in his condition.

I told him everything. My tears flowed unchecked and the tale was interspersed with my fears, my heartfelt apologies and my desires for his forgiveness. I professed my deep love for him, and I meant him no harm. I also told him my biggest fear was he would no longer be able to love our wee Josephine. My heart told me he wasn't such a man, but it seemed an awful thing to ask of any man. I explained it had been the deception which ate at my soul. I swore to him should I be so blessed to have him return to me I would never deceive him again and would accept the consequences. I lay my head upon his chest and sobbed until exhaustion overtook me. When I awoke a short time later, I felt an amazing physical lightness of being and seemed infused with hope that I could handle the future, no matter the outcome. I put his bedclothes to right and left to spend time with Jo in the garden.

In the afternoon, Henry came by as usual, and we sat down to go over the day's work. After a spell, I caught Henry looking at me.

"What? Why do you look at me so?"

"There's a difference in you today. You look younger, more energetic."

"Do I? Well, perhaps so. I've been having a bit of a struggle with the devil and I believe I won a major battle today." I smiled at him, placed my hand over his and said, "How could I lose when I have so many people like you who support and care for Thomas and me."

Then I simply bowed my head to the paperwork for we had just started to tackle a new project. It was a mystery we had noted while we had worked together on the company documents. There seemed to be a slow but steady increase in manifest items which were noted as lost or damaged during transit. We originally assumed it was due to some bad weather. However, we started keeping a keener eye out for such discrepancies and there was definitely an increase which had no bearing on weather, or shipping conditions.

"It is time for some quiet investigations on my part Fiona. If it were just one ship, I would be able to narrow it down quickly. However, it appears to be more random than it should. Let me pry about and get back to you."

Later. after supper, the girls were puttering about with the kitchen cleanup when Annie called me aside.

"Eh, Missus. I dinna know if ye care, but when I was in town this past noon, I saw quite a sight. Ye know the beggar what scared ye so? Well, there he was layin' in the street dead as a slaughtered pig. Seems he got into a fight and was knifed. I knew it was him as they hadn't carried his body off yet and no one bothered coverin' him. I ken yer not into gossip, but he seemed to frighten ye so, I thought you should know."

I'm glad I was seated as I felt the blood leave my face. The relief I felt was almost palpable for I had not really convinced myself he couldn't find me and Jo. I felt a twinge of guilt at thanking God for his death, but it was brief and gone with a silent "May God forgive him, for I could not."

"Thank you for telling me Annie. The man is undoubtedly better off as he looked to be a poor miserable creature." I went back to my duties thankful one more anxiety was lifted from my heart.

A couple of days later, I was tidying up Thomas's room and bringing clean linens and a washbowl since Peter would be coming up soon to bathe him and help me put on new bedclothes. Something made me look over at him and I saw his lovely brown eyes, bright and aware, looking directly at me with a slight smile on his lips.

Dropping what was in my arms, I ran to him. "Thomas, Thomas. You're back, oh Dear Lord, you're back."

"Hello Love," he whispered, "can I have a bit of water?"

I was crying and laughing with unbelievable joy as I helped him drink some water.

I didn't dare leave his room to tell the others for fear he would slip back into darkness. I simply went to the door and called for someone to come. Annie and Phoebe were there in moments and the both fell to their knees giving praises to God. They were simply reflecting exactly how I felt.

Phoebe asked if she could bring him anything. With a rather quizzical look on his face, he said,

"Now you mention it, I have an odd desire for some milk and a scone! Would that be possible?"

He was talking to empty air as Phoebe had left so quickly to do his bidding, there was nothing left but her shadow.

"Fi, what has happened? Why am I a bed when the last I remember was going to the office this morning? Why are my legs hurting so?"

I told him of the horrid accident, and he was shocked to learn he had been unconscious for over a week and semi-conscious for almost two.

"I seem to recall dreams where most of the time I was in darkness, as though I was living in the night sky, then sparks of lights, voices fading in and out. I felt indescribable pain but no way to cry out. Then, a long peace and I opened my eyes and saw you, my own private angel."

I gave him a quick summary of what brought this about, but there was so much to share, and he tired easily. So, just like the nourishment he needed, the information was doled out in small morsels.

As weak as he was, he was still getting stronger every day, and he insisted on working with Henry on some of the daily correspondence. He also tried to spend a bit of time each day writing. The damage to his hand did not prevent this, although it was painful, but the artistic script he was noted for was now a memory. He was also getting restless lying in bed all day and embarrassed to have to ask someone to assist him at the chamber pot. Peter, the gardener measured him to create a sturdy walking stick. It was then we fully realized just how badly his broken leg had healed. It was at least an inch shorter than his other leg. Clever Peter nailed on an extra piece of wood and leather on the heel of his boot to lessen the difference. He still had a noticeable limp, but could walk on his own, even though it was excruciatingly painful to do so. He could manage this for only a few steps at first but with a dogged determination he increased the distance daily.

He was quite fascinated by how we carried off our charade and made it seem Thomas was never out of commission and always in control. He thought sending Stanley on the ill-fated business trip to the Netherlands was a stroke of genius and it was wonderful to see the humor in his face at the retelling of the story. Stanley had recently returned, and Henry took great delight in listening to and sharing his rambling list of reasons why the negotiations failed, none of which, he assured Henry, was his fault.

"Fiona, I have been looking over the paperwork you and Henry have been doing for me while keeping my secret. To say I'm impressed would be an understatement! I can't even imagine how this would have turned out if you hadn't thought of, or been able to, maintain this deception. However, I think it's time we brought me back to the living and had a few people from the office see for themselves proof that I am alive and comparatively well, if not exactly kicking. Henry, perhaps you could arrange a business meeting here, so they see, even though I am damaged, I'm still in charge. I think a morning meeting would be best for I tire so easily. I am not at my best later in the day. I hate to ask, but I would also appreciate it if you two would continue your partnership in helping me with the work."

So, it was agreed to have the meeting, sooner, rather than later, and to continue on as before, but now with Thomas's wise counsel. About mid-day the day before the meeting, Henry burst into the house without even knocking, took the stairs two at a time and holding a sheaf of papers announced,

"Fiona! Thomas! I found it. I found the proof I needed to show our losses were not accidental."

He quickly brought Thomas up to speed on the mystery of the lost cargo and then explained,

"I've been hanging around the docks, staying quite well disguised and listening to the gossip. I then spent some time after hours in the office and found what I suspected. It seems our illustrious partner, Stanley Haverstead, has created a band of thieves, disbursed among several of our ships, who, stealing cargo, store it somewhere for Stanley to retrieve and sell later. Stanley then forges a new manifest showing those stolen goods as damaged, or lost at sea, and shares his profit with the brigands."

Thomas, clearly in shock, exclaimed. "I've never thought well of that sniveling little weasel but can't believe he would do something so underhanded to the company which handed him his job on a silver platter. How can you be sure it's Stanley behind this scheme?"

"Obviously the man is too cocksure of himself. He was even too lazy to carefully destroy the evidence. I found scraps of rough drafts of some of the latest forged manifests in his trash bin. I've brought them with copies of the originals. I guess he never thought anyone would think to ask our captains about their estimate of losses on a trip once those cargoes were off loaded!"

"Well then Henry, let's be sure Stanley is at our meeting on the morrow and I want you to use the opportunity to bring up our increase in losses. Don't make it sound as though you suspect foul play. I just want to observe his reaction. Let me look over your report and I'll decide what's to be done after the meeting."

"With your permission Thomas," Henry said, "I would also like to do one more thing. One of the ships in question is due in this afternoon. I would like to hang about and see if I can determine how the goods are taken."

"It's a good plan but be sure to be careful. If you're discovered it will not only upset our plans, you might be in real danger."

Smiling, he said he would, and Thomas might be surprised at just how scruffy he could look when he wanted to.

About 8:00 the next morning, Peter and Henry helped me prepare Thomas for his debut. I shaved and bathed him while Henry filled him in on his investigative adventure the previous afternoon. The doctor had given Thomas some powders to alleviate some of his constant pain, but Thomas seldom used it as he didn't like the way his brain was muddled and the odd dreams he suffered when asleep. Therefore, he took none this morning. The men got him dressed and moved him to a wooden chair with arm rests. I could tell by the tightness around his mouth the lifting and seating of him of caused him agony, but he said not a word. They carefully carried him to the parlor and tucked a blanket tightly round his legs. Everything he might need was placed on a table close enough so he could easily reach any of it during the meeting. By 9:00 a.m. the stage was set, and the attendees started to arrive. They were all polite and expressed much delight to see him, but the curiosity in the air was palpable. Thomas welcomed them with enthusiasm and his usual take charge energy. The wee dram of whiskey we gave him after breakfast did its job for there was a healthy high color in his cheeks! Thomas thanked all of them for all the hard work they had been doing in his absence, especially Henry for carrying on his usual duties and still taking time to run papers back and forth so he could continue his work while bedridden.

"The good news, boyos, is I shall be able to come back to the office soon. I'm a bit worse for wear but getting stronger every day!"

Clearing his throat, Stanley spoke up, "Well now, good to hear, good to hear. However, as hard as we've all had to work to make up for your absence, we were wondering if it might be best to have one of us take over your position, uh, you know, just, uh, until you are able to come back."

Several men seemed surprised at his remark and immediately disputed it, saying they thought all in all, the office ran quite smoothly with very little extra effort on their part. Stanley looked sullen but said nothing. They all continued discussing new contracts, ship repairs etc. When the meeting was almost over, at a nod from Thomas, Henry broached the key subject.

"As I mentioned before, Thomas, I'm still seeing an increase in losses due to damaged goods. I think we need to discuss possible reasons."

"Hmmm, yes. Gentlemen, it is worrisome. I believe most of the worst weather is over, so storms don't seem to be the problem. What think you?"

Someone asked if the ships had been checked for water tightness, another wondered if the cargoes were stored properly, or had the cargoes been checked at loading to be sure there was no shortage, or damage before shipping.

Frederick, the head clerk, spoke up, "Do you think there could be some dishonesty involved?"

Stanley who had been quite still and silent during this exchange suddenly seemed agitated and he was practically raising his hand like a schoolboy.

"Well! Before we start jumping to conclusions, I'd like to offer my services in looking over all of the documents and manifests to see if I can find any discrepancies."

Thomas, keeping a straight face, replied, "Stanley, what a generous offer and certainly not a bad idea. Well, let's finish this meeting and, if need be, we can meet here again in a couple of weeks, if I haven't been able to go to the office before then. Stanley, would you please remain for a bit so we can talk?"

Stanley practically simpered when agreeing to do so. The rest of the men left. Thomas purposefully poured a drink and handed it to Stanley who smugly sat back, took a sip and visibly relaxed.

"I do want to talk to you Haverstead, but not about investigating the losses. You see, we've already discovered the problem."

Stanley tilted his head quizzically.

"We have narrowed down the four ships which have had consistent losses and the men involved. You might be interested to know those men have already been placed on other ships sailing today. They have no knowledge of why the abrupt reassignment, but upon reaching their ports, they will be arrested by the masters at arms, who have letters from me to give to the local authorities."

Stanley's face was now the color of a halibut's underbelly and the hand holding the drink had developed a fine tremor.

"We have followed the cart your men used to hide the contraband and have officers protecting it in the warehouse you rented. Rather foolish of you to use your own name, but I could have identified you from the description they gave. Now, in deference to your uncle and the good name of the Company, I am not having you arrested, although a letter to do so has been written in case I change my mind. What I am going to do, is write a letter to the Board with my evidence and let them decide what to do with you."

"Oh, sweet Jesus!" I thought. The sniveling twit was starting to blubber.

"What? You can't. I-I m-m-mean...it's j-just that, that. No, please. Don't do that. I'll p-pay you back."

"You don't owe me Haverstead. You owe the Company, who gave you this position based on your uncle's say so. I'm sure your reputation and compensation for your theft will be much discussed prior to them meeting with you. Now, do me the greatest favor and get out of my home. Do not go back to the office and do not remove anything from the office. If you've something personal you need to retrieve, I'm sure Henry will be a gentleman and retrieve it for you. Should I hear of one single word said by you regarding this incident, I will immediately ensure the full story is made public and anyone who knows you at all will not doubt it."

Within days of the meeting, we could feel a busy, but peaceful pattern developing. Jo, of course was thrilled her Da was 'awake' and her buoyant sweet and optimistic personality blossomed again. His need to stay home was also a blessing as he could spend more time with her, and with me. Because even the hint of cold weather made his legs ache something fierce, we all spent more time in front of the fireplace. Soon after supper, Jo would curl up on the cushions and nestle against her Da with her special book. This was a rather impressive book on mythology telling the tale of Jason and the Argonauts. She and Thomas loved the story and never tired of reading it out loud. I would sit nearby doing some quiet work and listen as they took turns reading. The more often they read it, the more dramatically they did so. You would have thought they were performing at the Globe Theatre in London itself.

One evening Jo stopped reading and looked up at her father saying "I read this to you when you were sick, but I had to read all of the parts. Do you remember?"

His brow creasing, he tilted his head, "Yes. Yes, I believe I do. But I thought it was a dream. Why it was very kind of you my sweet little dove. Let's just read one more page as I see it is bedtime now. There's a good girl, now give me a kiss and hug. Jemma will be here soon to tuck you in."

After she was gone, I smiled at my husband and told him,
    "Oh Thomas, it pleased her so to think you heard her stories. I believe it helped her greatly to know she was doing something for you."

"Actually Fi, I do believe I heard her. I am starting to remember hearing and sensing things while I was in that state. I was sometime aware of whether the room was darkened or light. I heard voices, much as one might hear them standing outside a play, where the actor's voices come through the walls, but are muffled. I recall feeling jolts of pain, but almost as though it was happening to someone else. I must admit, it's all quite strange. I'm sure you spoke to me often, but I have no recollection of what you said, or even if I understood it at the time."

I sat very still with my work laying untouched in my lap. Nothing on his face gave me reason to believe he meant any more than he said. However, I was overcome with a clear and powerful message which simply said, "It is time."

"Thomas. I did speak to you, often, but I also confessed something to you. I know I felt it was safe to do so since you were not, well, not really present. However, I now know I must do so again as I have prayed and promised if I ever had a chance, I would tell you this story and put my faith in God and in our love."

It was easier this time and Thomas simply sat and listened quietly. When I told him of the rape, his fists clenched and tears shimmered on his lashes, but he remained silent. When I was done there wasn't a sound in the room until he quietly asked.

"Why did you not tell me Fiona?"

"Shame for what had happened, guilt for tricking you, but most of all fear. Fear you would reject me, but mostly fear you would reject Jo."

He sat with his head down for a long moment.

"Come here Fiona and sit on this stool." When I sat, he placed his hands on my shoulders, looked deeply into my eyes and explained, "I have always suspected something was amiss for I have seen you suffering inside, but I had no idea you had to deal with such a dreadful act. Then to try to find a way to resolve it by yourself. I think I am mostly hurt you didn't trust me enough to come to me. I have loved you from the time we were just children and I love you still. You did nothing wrong and you were only trying to find a solution in a world where a woman, no matter how much wronged, has few options. As far as Jo is concerned, she is the light of my life. She is proof God can take something as ugly as your assault and turn it into a blessing. Don't you see? We were meant to wed. It would have broken my heart to see you go to another man and as we saw, Fitzpatrick was no good option and proved to be a cold, cruel coward. We have also seen there seems to be a problem with us having another child, yet God gave us Jo and a sweeter child there couldn't be. I couldn't love her more than I do for, one way or another, she is ours from God."

He wrapped me in his arms, and I had never felt so loved, so safe and so blessed.

A special tranquility fell over our home and our life together took on a new closeness and level of trust which was so comforting. Thomas eventually went back to the office, but turned more and more of his duties over to Henry, so his days there were shorter. I was glad of his company as our time together grew ever more precious. It seemed releasing the chains of guilt I held so long opened a gate which let our love blossom and flow freely.

PROMISES KEPT – 1614 – ENGLAND AND HOME

At Christmastide, we received a long letter from Chloe. It was full of love and season's greetings, plus welcome news from home. Mam was doing well, though she spent most days dozing in the garden, or by a sunny window where she could watch for ships coming through the headlands. Periodically, she would ask when Da would be home, forgetting he had passed away three years ago, but would soon forget she asked.

With increased travel to and from the Americas, Mick was busy with the chandlery, which was now his. He had to struggle to find time to make repairs around our family home in Kinsale. Mick and Chloe said it was showing signs of not having a regular man around the house since Da died. Colum and Robbie were doing the Gearaghty name proud running the shipping business and raising fine families. Both had recently sent their eldest sons to school in Galway, which made Thomas smile with memories of his school days there. The most exciting news was Chloe was expecting a child in about six months. I was still heartbroken I hadn't been there for their wedding the previous year, but a series of storms made it too dangerous to attempt the trip. However, Thomas and I raised a glass to their blessed news. They had been hoping for children much sooner. Perhaps this would be the first of many. With all the little bits of information Chloe fit into the letter, Thomas and I had a most pleasant evening reading, re-reading and discussing all the details.

The next morning at breakfast, we started to talk about finances.

"Thomas. I know we send a generous amount home to help with expenses, but now I'm wondering if it will be enough. As Chloe's pregnancy advances, and after the babe is born, it will be difficult to run her own household, let alone run Mam's. Much of her time must be spent in caring for Mam's every need. I've often thought maybe it was a good thing she didn't have children yet. Do you recall she and Mick considered moving Mam in with them in Mick's cottage to make it easier, but it's just too small? If I recall, it's only three rooms."

"That's true. I was thinking of it too. I'm afraid they are going to have to consider hiring someone reliable to care for your mother and possibly have work done on the property. You know as well as I, the longer something goes unrepaired the worse it gets. When I get to the office, I'll look over our household books and see what we can do."

"Don't forget you also promised Jo a bigger boat for her twelfth birthday this summer! I'd hate to tell her we couldn't do so, but I trust her heart is kind enough she would understand why."

"Hmmm, I hadn't remembered my promise. I'll throw it into the pot as I figure out where we stand."

Giving me a warm kiss, he left, promising to pick up the discussion that evening.

Waiting until we were seated at supper, he broached the subject again by including Jo while discussing Chloe's letter and the good news about the babe. Then, he talked, in simple terms, about our concerns regarding Chloe and Mick possibly needing more financial help and why. Reaching across the table, he placed his hand over Jo's, looked into her eyes and asked,

"Jo. I would like to know if you could accept waiting for the new boat, I promised you if we need the money to help your Aunt Chloe and Uncle Mick?"

Her eyes grew large and I saw a lump in her throat when she swallowed. In a quavering voice, she whispered, "How long would I have to wait?"

"I'm not sure yet Love, but maybe even as long as a year."

She sat there quietly with her head down for moment. Raising it slowly, with unshed tears glistening in her eyes, she gave one quick, sharp nod and answered,

"I've told my friends about the boat, and I don't want to wait, but for you Da, I will."

I felt my throat tighten with pride in our girl and Thomas immediately got up and gave her a lovely hug and kissed the top of her little head.

"Alright then," he announced, with the boat situation settled I want you to know I have sent off several dispatches for I need more information before we make a decision. I have several ideas, each depending upon the information I receive. As it is Fiona, I sent some extra funds today to help your sister right away and make their Holiday's more cheerful."

This earned him his own hug and kiss! I also promised I would keep our personal expenses to a minimum. He smiled and told us he thought the three of us made quite a team.

The new year decided to bear down on us like a wild stallion. There was little traffic in and out of Portsmouth for almost two weeks while crews and every able-bodied man harbourside did their best to keep the ships moored and safe. They were bobbing about like corks and were off-loaded as quickly as possible. Of course, lightening their loads made them more buoyant and more likely to incur damage, but at least they didn't lose their cargoes to the deep waters. Thomas and all his staff were hard at work from dawn until deep into the frigid night. I could see the fatigue in Thomas's face when he would come home, eat whatever was placed in front of him and fall into bed.

We all woke on the morning of January 21st to gentle breezes, sunshine and the beautiful drip, drip of ice melting. Before Thomas left for work, all the household knelt and gave our heartfelt thanks to God. Later, Thomas came home and gave us the good news that there was much work to be done, but the damage to most of the ships was small compared to what it could have been. He said those who suffered the biggest losses were the ones who tried to leave the harbour during the storm and those who waited overly long to off-load their cargo.

Within five days Portsmouth was bustling again and Thomas was keeping regular hours. It was then when he surprised us with some additional news at supper.

"As you can well imagine, an impressive bundle of correspondence has landed on my desk in the past few days. In the stack were several responses to queries I made regarding our concerns over our family's needs in Kinsale. Hopefully they will give us the information we need to assist us in deciding how best to help them."

Looking at him hopefully, I asked, "Do you think we can do much more? Perhaps I can cut a bit further on the expenses."

Thomas smiled at me sweetly. "Now that is just what I would expect from you my love, but I don't see how you could do much more than you are now. However, after looking over the correspondence, I have changed my mind.

I could feel my face fall and tears sprang to my eyes. Jo looked at her father, then back at me, with some alarm. She was old enough to see my disappointment and to be surprised at the assumption our funds were stretched to their limit.

"No, no! It's not as bad as it sounds. It's just I have decided on a different plan, assuming you agree. Let me explain. I realized I have been working for the Company for just short of eleven years. During that time the Company has been setting aside a percentage of the profits attributed to the Portsmouth office. I asked them for an accounting, which I got in the post today. It can be ours within three months of my request for remittance. However once requested, the percentage clause ceases to exist. The amazingly wonderful new is it will be more than sufficient for us to do the following.

I will give the Company a three month notice of my intent to leave their employ and a recommendation of turning the management over to Henry Bell. Upon receipt of the funds, we will go home to be in lovely Kinsale, with those we love."

I ran to him, tear of joy streaming down my face, and held him with my face nestled against his neck.

"Let me go woman," he laughed, "I can hardly breathe. Sit here on my knee Sweetness, for I have more to tell. Jo, come over here too as I have another knee just for you. I also made an inquiry of our agent regarding the status of the cottage we had built. He accused me of being a mind reader as he had just spoken to the tenants about the annual rent coming due in February. He was going to write to tell me they were not planning on staying on as McCarthy's father had passed away and left him a small farm in Skibbereen. Apparently, they took excellent care of the cottage and the agent says we should have no problem getting another tenant. I don't think I want to rent it out again. What I want to do is ask the agent to get in touch with the stone mason who built it for us and ask him to add about three additional rooms to the structure. When it's done, I want to give it to Chloe and Mick!"

He gently reached for my chin and pushed it up to close my gaping mouth.

"Thomas! It is most generous of you, but if we did so we would no longer get an annual income from the cottage and even living in Mam and Da's house, we would still need funds on which to live. How can we afford to support ourselves?"

Reaching in the pocket of his jerkin, he handed me a letter with the broken seal of The Honourable East India Company. Unfolding it I glanced at a formal letter outlining the whys and wherefores of the funds they kept in trust for Thomas. I read and re-read the bottom line of the accounting. It must have been mis-written for it couldn't be right. My eyes reflected my confusion when I looked at him.

"Yes Fiona. The amount is exactly as written No one in our family need ever do without again. I would also ask that this number remain unknown to anyone outside of our solicitor for I want all to do their best based on their own merits before any assistance be considered. Your sister is different inasmuch as she and Mick have already done so much for your mother, therefore, they have earned the cottage. I will also ask Mick to hire out whatever needs to be done to put the family home to rights, as quickly as possible and to find a reliable and compassionate woman to care for your Mam so Chloe is freed up from taking on all the responsibility. Once we move in, you can decide if you wish to keep that woman on to help you with your mother."

Turning to Jo, he stated, "As for you my dearest one. I also have news. You shall have your new boat, but it will be built in Kinsale by the Irish who know the ways of the wild sea and the Bandon River. We will spend many a lovely day angling on the water and enjoying basket meals on the grassy shores.

" With a wink at me, he asked Jo, "Would such a life appeal to you Poppet?"

###

Made in the USA
San Bernardino, CA
07 November 2019